PROTECT THE ELEMENTALS

Piper stared at the gun the demon was holding on her, wondering if she could blow it up without letting the demon take her power and use it against her. She ultimately decided that a bullet would do less damage than an explosion.

"Look, witch," the demon said. "I don't care about you. Just let me have the Earthshaker and you can go on your merry way."

"I think we both know that's not going to happen," Piper replied, shifting her body so she was in front of Muriel. If she had to, she could try to freeze time if the gun was fired. Maybe if she just tried to freeze the bullet and not the demon she wouldn't have her power reflected back. Of course, the idea of freezing a bullet heading at her at the speed of, well, a speeding bullet, was no easy task. Then again, it was better than the other option: death.

THE BREWING
STORM

An original novel by Paul Ruditis

Based on the hit TV series created by

Constance M. Burge

New York   London   Toronto   Sydney

Prologue

It was a dark and stormy midafternoon.

In fact, it was much darker and far stormier than it should have been for San Francisco in early fall. For days the weather had been unseasonable to say the least. The five-day forecast had looked like an encyclopedia of climatic terminology and every day brought new weather anomalies that couldn't have been predicted.

It started harmlessly enough on Monday with the typical morning fog, which spread over the entire city and stayed all day in spite of the wild winds blowing out of town. Tuesday brought searing heat and humidity, yet somehow managed to drop below freezing by nightfall. Wednesday saw more wind, with the addition of hail that pelted the area and covered the ground six inches deep. People were still shoveling out from under the ice on Thursday when snow came down on top of it.

wet road. He was able to right the car and get it into the lot with only minimal damage to the passenger side door as he scraped past the gate.

The demons had been impossible to shake on the road. However, Christopher suspected that heading out on foot wasn't going to be any better. He hoped that he'd have an advantage out in the elements, or at least that the demons would have a disadvantage tracking him. Fleeing to the safety of his own home was not an option, because that was exactly what they wanted him to do, and the police weren't really much help when demons were involved.

He pumped his brakes and finally came to a safe stop straddling a couple of parking spots. There were only a few cars in the lot. Before he turned off the engine, he saw that the clock on the dashboard showed it was just after four. He was supposed to be on the air in an hour giving the latest update on the weather that had been plaguing the city.

Somehow he didn't think he was going to make that broadcast.

Christopher dashed out of his car, making sure to grab his cell phone as he went for the path to the Golden Gate Bridge. At the same time, the demons came to a screeching halt behind him. For a brief moment Christopher wondered where the demons had gotten a car from in the first place, but figured that simple theft was nothing compared to attempted murder. He hit

He briefly considered using his powers against the demons, but knew that would be playing right into their hands. An indirect attack could backfire with all the people around, especially considering that his intense fear would probably mess with his control. Christopher was out of options, but took solace in the fact that they had the kid to fall back on.

The demons weren't as close as he originally thought, but they were certainly closing in. They were big, scary, human-looking demons, built more for battle than for speed. One rather formidable woman led three hulking men toward him. They weren't running so much as walking quickly, and Christopher couldn't help but wonder why the bad guys never seemed to run, as if speed walking was somehow more menacing. He wished he was going to have time to figure that little mystery out.

He wished he had more time to do a lot of things.

Christopher considered flagging down a car, but figured even if a driver was going to be kind enough to give the sweating, panting, slightly rain-soaked man with crazed fear in his eyes a ride, that same driver would probably not stop in the middle of the bridge to do so. It wouldn't help in the long run anyway. He knew there was only one way out of this.

At least he had the chance to choose how he died.

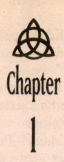

Chapter

1

A beam of sunlight streamed through the frost on the kitchen window of Halliwell Manor and fell perfectly onto the notepad beside the stove. With a pencil in one hand, Piper Halliwell was adding ingredients to the list from memory. Her other hand was busy slowly stirring a steaming pot in a counter-clockwise direction with a long wooden spoon. She put a check mark next to each item on the list as she confirmed the ingredients carefully laid out before her in a precise fashion. There was little room for error—everything had to be measured out exactly and added in the proper timeframe. The steam rising from the pot had a pleasant aroma, a sign she was on the right track.

"Hey there," her half-sister Paige Matthews said as she came into the kitchen and took in the scene. "Potion?"

"Potatoes," Piper replied as she picked up the

"Yes, darling," Leo said in a forced pleasant tone as he entered the kitchen.

Piper knew that she was on the verge of trying his patience—actually, she suspected that she had already crossed that line a few minutes ago—but she couldn't worry about that right now. When she got into full-on cooking mode it tended to occupy her mind one hundred percent. It had been a while since she had gotten into it this deeply, but that's what the day was supposed to be about. She had even taken the night off from work so she could enjoy the meal she'd be taking all day to prepare.

That was one of the perks of owning her own club. She was able to take off whenever she wanted, even though Saturday was typically the busiest night of the week. She also liked the fact that she got to see the hottest bands for free, as P3 was turning into quite the little hot spot. The club's success was one of the reasons she needed to take the day off, since with her other responsibilities she hadn't scheduled any time for herself in what seemed like forever.

"I need you to go over to the store again and pick up some pistachios . . . shelled if they have them . . . please?"

"Are you sure that's all that you need," Leo asked, and quickly added, "sweetheart? Maybe you could go online and check out the recipe there."

"Wow, I thought cooking was supposed to calm people," Paige said as Piper abruptly hung up the phone and took the spoon back.

"I used to love to cook," Piper said. "Hated working for a prissy restaurant manager, but loved the cooking part. Now I hardly have any time to make anything aside from anti-demon potions. And now that my recipes are gone—"

"You figured it was time to start up again—"

"Trying to recreate the recipes from memory," Piper said. "But guess what? My memories just aren't what they used to be. Wonder why. My body's only been taken over by other beings how many times?"

Piper actually stopped to think about that for a moment. Considering the high number of entities always trying to control them or kill them, Piper was actually surprised that she was able to take any time off to cook at all.

Then the phone rang again.

Oh, I'm sorry, she thought. *What time off?*

Paige started to move toward the cordless.

"Leave it," Piper said. "It's been ringing all morning."

"I know, I heard it up in the attic," Paige said. "What's going on?"

As if for emphasis, the phone rang again.

"The storm knocked out the electricity at P3 last night in the middle of the band's set," Piper explained. "There was some kind of power surge that blew out one of the amps, which the writing. You know . . . public appearances, interviews. We're even talking about doing some endorsements. I'm thinking maybe I should get an agent . . . and a business manager."

"Wow, aren't we just the movers and shakers," Paige said. "I feel like such a sloth."

"Hey," Piper said, throwing her arm around her sister. "You do important work at the center. You know that."

"I know," Paige said. "I just think there's got to be something else out there for me. Besides, I've really been so focused on magic lately that it seems like my attention's been split."

"Speaking of which," Phoebe said as she grabbed a breakfast bar from the cabinet, "find anything on that weird weather stuff yet? The storm kept me up half the night. On the bright side, I did have time to go over my contract. Good thing, too. The lawyers tried to slip in some 'morals clause' that actually said that as their representative, my behavior outside the office had some kind of bearing on the 'Ask Phoebe' persona I had created, and I would have to conduct myself responsibly or suffer some kind of legal consequences that I don't actually understand."

Piper took a taste of her stew and sprinkled in another dash of curry. Her mind flashed back to her late sister Prue. The more Phoebe got into her job, the more she sounded like the career-driven, ever-efficient, eldest Halliwell—although Piper that Darryl Senior and his lovely wife, Sheila, could have a romantic weekend (mostly) to themselves. The only problem was that a massive storm had hit the previous night, scaring the boy so much that he refused to leave the house even though his dad assured him that he would be safe in the car. Darryl couldn't blame his son, though. At times the intensity of the lightning and thunder had even scared him, but since it's not usually reassuring to know that anything scares your dad, Darryl had kept that part secret. That's why he found himself taking a detour on the way to work that morning, the last day of his six-day shift.

Darryl slid into his chair and surveyed the neatly organized stacks of paperwork surrounding him. He wasn't usually the type to let work get backed up like this, but in recent years his reports had begun taking longer and longer to prepare since so much of the paperwork had to be fabricated. That was another thing Darryl didn't use to do—lie with such ease to so many people. But he knew he could never reveal the truth behind many of the cases he worked on. Too many lives depended on that.

It wasn't that Darryl liked lying in his official paperwork; he just had no choice in the matter. Aside from the potential for saving lives by distorting the truth, the real story was usually too extraordinary to believe. Witches, demons, and magic were still largely in the closet in fairly liberal San Francisco, which is but he would certainly never get used to it or the part he played in it all.

"Hey, Inspector," Detective Warrington called to Darryl from her desk across the room. "What's with this freaky weather? Doesn't have anything to do with a case you're working on, does it?"

Darryl simply smiled and shook his head. He didn't have an active case at the moment, but that wasn't the point of the joke. Around the office, Darryl was getting quite the reputation for his involvement in weird—some might say "paranormal"—cases, which made his reports all the more difficult to write.

"Yeah, Morris," her partner, Detective Simpson, added. "Is there some Oogidy-Boogidy making all this rain?"

"Is Zeus throwing around all this lighting?" Warrington asked.

"Is Jack Frost nipping at your nose?" Simpson added as the duo cracked themselves up.

"Very funny," Darryl said, though he was thoroughly *un*amused, and quietly surprised that Warrington knew Zeus was the Greek God credited with using lightning to make a point.

"We've got one here for you," Simpson added. "Happened yesterday afternoon. Seems we got a jumper off the Golden Gate. Hey, now that I think of it, he was a *weatherman* on the local news."

"Nothing new about a jumper," Darryl replied as he got up to deliver his report to the chief.

know they aren't the best at handling the press."

"They need the practice," the chief admitted, but implied that this would be the case they would get that practice on.

"It sounds kind of odd," Darryl replied, still searching for a way to insert himself into the investigation. "Don't you think?"

"No odder than the stuff you've been getting into lately," the chief said. There wasn't any accusation in his voice. Darryl knew the chief had been on the force for years and had seen many strange things in that time. San Francisco wasn't one of the most conservative cities to begin with. Of course, he also knew the chief was only going to turn a blind eye for so long.

"I've got something else for you," the chief said as he handed Darryl a note. "Call just came in on a missing kid. Seems pretty normal . . . at least as normal as any sicko who would take a kid."

"I'll get right on it," Darryl said as he turned and left the chief's office. As much as he hated working kidnapping cases, he was actually looking forward to a normal case for once, dealing with normal police work, normal suspects, and normal leads.

The problem was that he couldn't get his mind off the *ab*normal case he had just heard about. As he walked through the station he made a mental note to check in with the Charmed Ones about the exploding jumper.

missing kid yet, so the case could go either way, and runaways had slightly better odds than kidnap victims.

Stephen and Maria Michaels hadn't even known their child for a full year. He had only just officially become their son earlier in the week, and they were moved beyond words by his disappearance. The vibe Darryl was getting was that the parents weren't involved in any foul play, as the saying goes. Unfortunately, in these situations it was the parents who got the first pass as possible suspects.

Darryl hated that part of the process— examining everything the parents said and did. He couldn't imagine how he would behave if he ever walked into his son's room to find the boy missing. He didn't *want* to imagine it, either.

"Mrs. Michaels," Darryl said.

"Maria, please," she replied as she gathered herself together.

"When did you finally check on him?" Darryl continued to gently prod for answers.

"About a minute before we called the police," Maria replied, her hands had reached for the nearest throw pillow and were twisting it at the edges.

"Shortly after nine," Stephen added softly.

"I could just tell something was wrong," his wife continued. "The bed was a mess . . . there were things strewn all over his desk. He's been

Darryl was preparing himself to ask the next set of difficult questions when he heard someone clearing her throat behind him. He turned to see Officer McGee standing in the foyer.

"Excuse me for a minute," Darryl said quietly as he got off the couch and went to join the officer.

"Sorry to interrupt," McGee said in a tone that matched the silence in the house. Everyone was speaking in hushed voices as if it were a library . . . or a morgue. "But I think you're needed outside."

There was something about McGee's strained tone and stiffened body language that set Darryl immediately on alert. He gave a glance back to Mr. and Mrs. Michaels and threw in a silent look of apology before he stepped outside onto the front patio. He immediately saw why McGee had been so tense.

A pair of dark sedans was parked on the opposite side of the street. The cars so obviously belonged to the FBI that Darryl was surprised he didn't see the initials emblazoned in white on the hoods. One man sat behind the wheel of the first car looking up at the house, while another pair of agents sat in the second car. The lead investigator was making his way up the steps to the patio.

"I certainly hope the SFPD didn't contaminate my crime scene," the Fed said as he approached Darryl with a sneer on his face that made McGee's body tense up even further, if that was possible.

never was one of those bureaucrats who came in claiming jurisdiction and kicking out the local police, which was probably why most of the times he and Darryl worked together had been successful.

"Do you have a read on the situation yet?" Harkins asked. "Gut feeling?"

"Too early," Darryl replied. "I was just getting to the fun part," he added sarcastically.

"Shall we?" Harkins pointed toward the open door.

Darryl nodded to McGee to stay out on the patio while he led Harkins into the house and briefed the agent on the little he knew so far. When they reached the living room they found Mrs. Michaels still sitting on the couch digging her nails into the throw pillow, already wearing a hole in the chenille. Mr. Michaels had moved over to his desk, where he seemed to be contemplating whether to smoke a cigarette. The open pack was in his hand, but he hadn't pulled one out yet.

"Sorry," he said, putting the pack down. "I've been trying to quit. This is my emergency pack. Figured this is an emergency." But he walked away from the cigarettes and joined his wife back on the couch.

"Mr. and Mrs. Michaels, this is Federal Agent Sam Harkins," Darryl said, introducing the new player. "He and his team will be taking over the investigation."

unusual difficulties with the adoption? Maybe with his birth parents?"

"So far as we know, they're out of the picture," Stephen replied. "Tyler's been shuttled around from foster home to foster home for years."

"There *was* some problem with the last home," Maria added. "The parents just suddenly disappeared."

Darryl exchanged a glance with Harkins. That was a route definitely worthy of pursuit, though Darryl couldn't help but think back to earlier in the morning when he was dealing with another kind of mysterious disappearance.

"What do you mean by 'disappeared'?" Harkins asked.

"We're not sure," Maria replied, ripping into the fabric of the pillow. "Tyler never wants to talk about it."

"Maybe you should talk to the social worker who put us together with Tyler," Stephen suggested. "I always got the feeling that she knew more about the situation but for whatever reason she wouldn't—or couldn't—tell us."

At the mention of the social worker, Darryl's intuition went on high alert. Since there were probably hundreds, if not thousands, of social workers in the city, the odds were slim that his suspicions would prove true. However, the idea that popped into his head probably had something to do with the fact that they had also referred to people mysteriously disappearing.

Renegotiating her contract was only one of the things on Phoebe's mind. Growing up, she had never imagined herself being "contracted" to work anywhere. It just seemed so permanent, and in a way it was. Once she signed that piece of paper, she would be legally locked into her job for whatever period of time they mutually agreed upon.

Phoebe knew that it wasn't like she was signing her soul away. That was probably something more in line with her other, more magical, line of work. There was just something that seemed so *final* about what she was doing. No matter how much she liked the work and the attention it brought her, there was something intimidating about the possibility of doing this for the rest of her life.

In addition to the unexpected contract renegotiation, Phoebe was also dealing with the added responsibilities of interviewing for an assistant, figuring out her health insurance, and starting up a retirement plan. If that last part didn't make her feel old, she didn't know what would. Add her recent divorce from Cole to that list and she was feeling prematurely aged.

Well, here I go, she thought as she took a deep breath and enjoyed the last bit of sunshine before entering her fog-enshrouded workplace.

"There you are," her editor, Elise Rothman, said before Phoebe even stepped into the office's bull pen. "I swear I'm going to have you hooked with what she had been up to when she used to ditch chemistry with Josh Login in high school. Somehow, she had managed to become that which she always feared: a grown-up.

"I actually need to talk to you about an entirely different matter." Elise took a seat in Phoebe's guest chair.

Phoebe had hoped she could get to work on either the article or the contract as soon as she got in the office. Once Elise sat, she knew both of those things had just gotten back-burnered. She took a seat at her desk. "Yes?"

"I know your column keeps you very busy," Elise said. "But I was hoping you could help me out of a little jam."

"Oh, Elise, you know I'll be happy to do anything," Phoebe said, then added, "if I can."

"This is right up your alley," Elise quickly added with a wave of her hand as if it was nothing. "You see, Granny Goodwords had to take a short sabbatical."

"Granny Goodwords?"

"Our children's advice columnist for the Sunday supplement," Elise said as if Phoebe should know what she was talking about. "Kids write to her asking for help with their little problems, like 'My friend keeps teasing me,' 'My brother ripped off my favorite doll's head' . . . that kind of thing. Granny Goodwords tells them how to handle the situation."

"Uh-huh," Phoebe said, surprised to find that

boy, Phoebe discreetly glanced down at her shiny silver letter opener and tried to angle the metal so she could see her reflection. With all the contracts and retirement funds conversations of late, combined with being asked to take on the role of a "Granny," she wasn't surprised when she thought she saw the beginnings of wrinkles around her eyes.

"Phoebe?" Elise asked.

Phoebe slammed the letter opener down on her desk when she realized that Norah had left the room and Elise was staring at her.

"Kidnapping?" she asked, hoping to keep the subject off herself for a moment. There wasn't a doubt that she would help Elise, but she wanted to get used to the whole "Granny" thing first.

"Or a runaway," Elise replied. "We don't know yet. Right now it's just a missing boy. . . . You know, I remember a time when I never referred to these stories as *just* a missing child. Maybe I'm getting jaded. Or maybe it's just the way I cope with it."

Phoebe knew what Elise was talking about. After saving so many innocents she certainly was more used to the idea, but she also knew that each one was important. She hoped that she'd never lose that feeling.

"I'm sure at some point in the day it'll hit me," Elise continued. "And my mind will get stuck on whatever could be happening to poor little Tyler Michaels."

had never realized it would. Instead of seeing it for the success that it was, she could only see the adoption as a near failure of the system solely because she couldn't explain the fact that the boy's last set of foster parents had been a pair of demons trying to corrupt him into becoming a bodyguard for The Source.

When Paige had met Tyler, she had seen him as a kindred spirit because he was also learning about a power he never knew he had. He was a Firestarter on the run from his foster demons. Paige took him home, where Tyler immediately bonded with the family, especially Piper. And once they saved the day, Paige made it her mission to find him a good family.

It didn't take long for Paige to come across Stephen and Maria Michaels, but it sure took forever to get them to be Tyler's parents. The time she spent working the case was time she knew should have been spent learning more about her new life as a Charmed One, but she certainly wasn't going to let Tyler slip through the cracks in the system. More and more she was considering taking a break from work to focus on learning about her magic, but she couldn't stop thinking about what she would do once she got past her studies.

Paige didn't want to be a burden, but she also didn't know what she wanted to be when she grew up, as the saying goes. That fear of her future was the one thing keeping her at her job,

"I'm sorry," Piper said. "But I really want this meal to be perfect. They keep calling from the club and I guess I was getting distracted and something just wasn't right. . . ."

"Piper," Leo said, carefully choosing his words. "It's your first day off in . . . what . . . decades? Maybe you should try . . . I don't know . . . relaxing?"

"I cook to relax," she replied simply. "Don't I seem relaxed?"

As if an answer to Piper's own question, the phone rang and, without even looking, she thrust out her hand and blew it up.

"Okay," she said, taking a deep breath. "I promise I will relax once I get started on the main course. But before I can do that, I need you to go to the store . . . please."

"You know, my powers really are supposed to be used for more productive purposes," he replied. "I'm not your mystical errand boy."

"No, you're my wonderfully sweet and understanding husband," Piper said, buttering him up. "Who has one heck of a gourmet dinner in his future, if only he'll go to the store for me one more time."

Leo gave her a look of exasperated resignation that silently told her that the dinner had better be really good and include one very rich and decadent dessert.

"I love you," Piper replied. She then handed over the newest list and watched him orb off.

"I love you, too," Paige said as she came

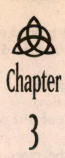

Chapter

3

The upper-level demon known as Tempest leaned back in his stone chair and looked down at the minion who knelt before him. The chair was raised up on a platform specifically so the minion had to lift his head even higher to see his master towering above him, which was really the point of the layout of the entire room.

It was all Tempest could do to make the place more comfortable for himself.

It wasn't really a prison so much as a safe haven, as far as the demon was concerned. True, it was a safe haven he could leave only once a century, but he tried to focus on the positive. There was so much about the room to hate.

The room was actually more of a cave. But instead of an interestingly murky and damp cave that chilled him to the bone, the place was always kept pleasantly at room temperature.

"Oh, great and powerful one," the minion said.

"Enough with the empty praise," the demon replied. "My ego is fine, really. Move it along."

"I am so sorry for this failure," the minion continued, bowing repeatedly as he spoke.

"I'm getting seasick," Tempest said. "Stand up straight. Be a demon."

"Yes, master," the minion replied.

Ego aside, Tempest did like the "master" part.

"I am so sorry for failing you once again," the minion continued. "It was beyond my control. I was unprepared for what was waiting. That is no excuse, but I beg your forgiveness."

Tempest paused to let his minion sweat the moment. He picked up the file on the table beside his chair and flipped through it. Yesterday's "failure," as the minion had put it, was actually a success. Not only was their prey dead, but they also managed to get a very important piece of information. The file was incredibly thorough and had already proved to be very useful. It did have one rather important omission, but his minion had found that out earlier, so he figured that they were back ahead of the game.

"Okay," Tempest said.

"Okay, master?" the minion asked.

"Okay, I accept your apology," Tempest replied simply. "What, did you think I was going to kill you or something?"

"Well . . . yes," the minion said. The relief was evident on his face.

"Leave something off the list?" Leo asked as he orbed back into the kitchen. Then he saw Tyler sitting at the table drinking hot chocolate beside Paige. "Hey, Tyler. I didn't know you were coming by . . . in your pajamas?"

Tyler just stared into his hot chocolate.

"So far, our best guess is sleepwalking," Paige said. "Tyler's been kind of mum on the subject."

Piper pulled Leo off to the side so they could talk quietly, as if Tyler wouldn't know they were talking about him.

"He just showed up and wouldn't say a word," she whispered. "But we can see the fear in his eyes. Not to mention the whole sleepwear ensemble."

"Maybe we should call his parents," Leo suggested.

"Before we know what's going on?" Piper asked. "They don't know anything about his powers."

"Well, they must know something's wrong," Leo said. "They're probably worried sick."

"And if we call them, they'll insist on coming over here," Piper said. "By the time they get here, who knows what they could walk into? I promised Tyler a normal life."

"And we'll do our best to help him have it," Leo said, putting an arm around her. "But we're not going to be able to do anything about it if he won't tell us what's going on."

"Maybe he just needs a few minutes," Piper said. "I'm sure he'll open up to me."

one," Piper said as she sat next to her young friend.

Tyler took another sip of his hot chocolate. "I thought it was all supposed to stop," he said. "Once you took away my powers."

"Tyler, I didn't *take* your powers," Piper corrected him. "You've still got them. You just can't use them right now."

"Is that why they came after me?" he asked.

"Who?" Piper asked, her defenses immediately raised. "Who came after you?"

"I don't know," Tyler said, pushing aside his mug. "I woke up this morning and there was this guy holding me down."

"Did he look like a normal guy?" Phoebe asked as she took a seat at the table. "Or did he look kinda demony?"

"Demony?" he asked.

"You know," Paige said. "Horns . . . glowing eyes . . . a tail . . . all of the above."

"He looked normal," Tyler replied, which didn't really prove anything. Most of the demons they dealt with took on human form. "He kept pushing down on my chest. And he was mumbling . . . about not failing again or something. I thought that Source thing wasn't supposed to be interested in me anymore."

"You don't have to worry about him right now. He's not in the picture," Paige said. "Or, wait . . . is he back again? I lose track."

Piper ignored her sister. "Tyler, I don't think it

I opened the window, climbed down the tree, and ran."

"All the way here?" Phoebe asked. "That's over a mile."

"It's not that far," Tyler said as if he did it all the time. "I know the demon followed me out of the house, but I'm pretty sure I lost him. I had to keep hiding to make sure he wasn't following me." He looked back out the window to check for demons.

"I'm sure no one did," Piper said quickly. "Or they would have grabbed you before you got in the house. "You're safe here."

"First thing we have to do is let your parents know you're here," Paige said.

"We can't," Phoebe jumped in. "If my paper's got a reporter at his house then there have to be about a dozen others. Add to that the cops and maybe even the FBI, and I don't see how we can get a message to them without bringing a ton of people to our door."

"I think we have to focus on finding out who's after him," Leo suggested. "Once we take care of the problem we can get Tyler home."

"Quick, to the batcave," Paige said as they got up, moving to the attic and the Book of Shadows.

Piper took Tyler by the hand and led him out of the room. She took a quick glance back to her bare stovetop, knowing the odds of getting any more cooking in today were slim to none. She

Darryl knew all about the Charmed Ones' more secret activities, they were always reluctant to get the inspector involved. Sometimes he appreciated being ignorant, while other times . . . not so much.

"Can I come in?" Darryl asked when she failed to offer.

"Sure, sure," Phoebe said quickly, and waved him into the house. "So what brings you here on a Saturday morning?"

"Phoebe," Darryl said. "I'm going to ask you a question right now, and the answer is 'no', okay?"

Phoebe looked at him questioningly. "Okaaay."

"Here, let's rehearse it," he added. "Say it with me now . . ."

"No," they said in unison.

Even though she was playing along, Phoebe's face registered concern along with her confusion.

"Good," he said. "Now, I'm working on a missing child case, and your sister's name came up during the investigation. You wouldn't happen to have seen a Tyler Michaels recently."

Phoebe looked up at Darryl, but did not respond.

"Okay, this is the part where you say 'no,'" Darryl said, as if she needed prodding.

Phoebe easily could have done as he asked, but she hated lying to Darryl. She especially hated the idea of him chasing leads all over the

Leo standing in the middle of the attic with the missing child in question. The smile that was on Tyler's face in the photo his parents had showed Darryl was long gone. In its place was a look quite similar to that which Darryl's own son had worn on his face during the previous night's storm. Darryl's hope that it was just a simple runaway situation disappeared when he saw Paige flipping through the Book of Shadows.

"Hey, Darryl, how's it going?" Leo asked.

"Well, let's see," Darryl said. "Half the force and the FBI are currently scouring the city for that boy standing right next to you. So I'd say things are about par for the course."

Tyler took a step closer to Piper.

"Tyler, this is our friend Darryl," Piper said in a calm and reassuring tone. "He's a police officer."

"Don't worry," Phoebe added. "He's one of the good guys."

"Thanks," Darryl said sarcastically as he nodded hello to Tyler. He knew why Phoebe had said what she said, but still hated the fact that more and more often it seemed that people had to point out when the police were on their side.

Tyler gave a tentative smile in response.

"Hail, hail, the gang's all here," Paige mumbled as she flipped to the page about Firestarters. She was actually glad that Darryl had showed up, because it was easier to have the police around on those occasions when you also had the police looking for the person standing in

Everyone in the room gave her a curious look.

"What? I've always been interested in Ancient Greece," she replied defensively. "I love that time in history with the art, the science . . ."

"The simple, yet elegant fashions," Paige added.

"Can I help it if I look good in well-draped sheets?" Phoebe replied slyly.

"Yeah, okay, we'll get you an outfit for your birthday," Piper said, trying to rush things along. "What's with this Night of Aeolus, Paige?"

Paige flipped through the book and found an entry she had never seen before. That wasn't much of a surprise, since the dearly departed Halliwell women were always adding things to the book when needed. Paige scanned through the text.

"Well, this would have been useful a week ago," Paige said. "The Night of Aeolus is pretty much the entire reason the weather has been so freaky lately."

continued to read. "'On the Night of Aeolus, by the light of the full moon, the elements must come together to set everything in its proper place. To do this, a Firestarter"—she nodded in Tyler's direction—"is charged with gathering other Elementals at the Circle of Gaea to perform the Ritual of the Guardians.'"

Tyler looked even more worried. "What are Elementals? Does that mean there are others like me?"

"Well, we knew that Firestarters were rare, but it didn't mean you were the only one," Piper said.

"I don't think it's just other Firestarters," Phoebe added. "I think it means people who can control the other elements."

"Other elements?" Tyler asked.

"Earth, wind, and water," Phoebe explained.

"Earthstarters?" Tyler asked, making a lame attempt at a joke to lighten the mood for himself more than anyone. "That sounds stupid."

"I'm sure they have some other name," Piper said, playing along. "So I guess we have to help Tyler collect the other Elementals. When is this Night of Aeolus?"

"Um . . . ," Paige replied. "Tonight."

"Tonight?" Piper repeated as she joined her sister at the book. "Then why didn't Grams or someone add this little tidbit to the book earlier? We could have been working on this all week. It's not like we've got a bunch of time to run to the book," Phoebe said, looking down at Tyler. "I don't think Tyler was supposed to be involved in the ritual . . . and neither were we."

"What do you mean?" Darryl asked. "What's going on now?"

Phoebe looked down at the boy again. "Tyler, why don't you go downstairs and pour yourself some more hot chocolate."

Tyler looked up at Phoebe—well, technically, due to an early growth spurt, he was almost as tall as her and pretty much looked her directly in the eyes. "Do you really think what you're going to say is any worse than the things I'm going to think of if I'm *not* in the room?"

"Smart kid," Paige said.

"Phoebe, what did you see?" Piper asked, obviously agreeing with the boy. "Was it Tyler's future?"

"No," Phoebe replied. "It didn't involve Tyler at all. Not directly, at least. I saw some guy . . . I think it was the weather guy on San Fran News . . . I saw him jump off the Golden Gate Bridge and . . . he kinda . . . exploded before he hit the water."

"I know about that," Darryl said. "But it happened yesterday. That's not in the future."

"Yeah, welcome to my wacky power," Phoebe said.

"But why are you seeing some other guy when you touched Tyler?" Paige asked.

"Sounds like he was a Firestarter too," Leo

through the book. "Let's see . . . Tempest . . . Tempest . . . I have a *Tempus*."

"Been there, vanquished him," Piper said.

Paige continued flipping, "Here we are . . . Tempest. . . . Oh, this is *so* not good."

"Of course not," Phoebe mumbled.

"Give us the Cliff's Notes version," Piper said.

"Well, in short, Tempest is *all* about controlling the weather," Paige said.

"Yeah, we got that part," Phoebe interrupted. "Jump to the good stuff."

"He was banished to a neutral environment that he can only leave on the Night of Aeolus," Paige continued. "Tempest commands a quartet of demons with the ability to drain the powers of Elementals. . . . Oh, and look at this, they can absorb witches' powers too. Goody. . . . Anyway, if the powers can be collected from four Elementals by the Night of Aeolus, they will transfer those powers to their master, and he will be able to control the weather all over the world."

"I'm guessing it was one of his minions in Tyler's room this morning," Leo said.

"But he couldn't drain anything because Tyler's powers are bound," Piper added.

"So this Tempest guy has demons that run around and do the dirty work for him?" Darryl asked. The question was mostly rhetorical because he was regretfully familiar with the tendency of the demon community to rely on lackeys.

"Hey, Piper, how about some of that stew before we get to work," Paige said. Piper just glared in response. "Okay, maybe later."

And just like that, the five adults in the room started talking about what to do and how to do it. Their cross talk was fast-paced and utterly confusing, based on conjecture and assumptions that weren't leading them anywhere. But that all stopped once Tyler spoke up.

"Umm," he said tentatively. "Can I have my powers back?"

"What?" Piper asked. "Why?"

"So I can protect myself," Tyler said.

"But we can protect you," Piper replied. "Like we did last time."

"Actually, honey," Leo said. "I think he protected us a bit too."

"I promise I won't use them unless I have to," Tyler said.

"I think he's going to need them tonight anyway," Phoebe added.

Piper thought it over for a moment. When they first met, she had been so much in favor of allowing him to grow up with his power remaining active, it was odd that she was reluctant to give it back to him. It was just that she had gotten so used to the idea of Tyler having a normal life that she didn't want to put that in jeopardy. Then again, it looked like the fates were conspiring against that normal life happening this weekend.

"Fire extinguisher!" Paige called out, and a moment later the item appeared in her hand. She sprayed down the fire calmly, having burned a few things herself in her own exploration of magic.

"Sorry," Tyler said sheepishly. "I was just trying to make a little fire, like a candle."

"It's okay," Piper said. "Your power has been dormant for a while. It makes sense that it would come on a little strong the first time you used it. I should have warned you about that."

"Maybe someone should open a window," Phoebe suggested as the room filled with smoke and the smell of the extinguisher's chemicals.

"Got it," Darryl said as he moved toward the nearest window and opened it, letting in some fierce breezes. He leaned out for some fresh air and saw something that made him pull himself right back into the room.

"What is it?" Piper asked when she saw his very sudden movement.

"We've got company," he replied as the doorbell rang.

walk," Darryl said, his mind working on the problem. There was really no reason Harkins had to come in the house that he could think of. "Don't know if he saw me, but I'm not willing to play those odds with Tyler up here. He's probably just checking out Paige's connection to Tyler. Let's not give him a reason to get suspicious."

"Okay," Paige said as she came around from behind the Book of Shadows. "I'll go downstairs with Darryl. You guys stay up here with Tyler and try to be quiet."

As they started down the stairs, Darryl prepped Paige for what to expect. "He'll probably ask when you last saw Tyler and what kind of mood he's been in."

"It was earlier this week," Paige said. "When we finalized the adoption papers. And, aside from the whole being-chased-by-demons thing, he's been a pretty happy kid. I assume he'll ask about the fact that Tyler's last set of foster parents went suspiciously missing."

"Yeah, and if we can avoid telling him that they were blown up, or melted, or split into a thousand tiny particles, that would be best," Darryl said, trying to lighten the mood. He knew Paige would be fine answering Harkins's questions. All three of the Charmed Ones were good at explaining the unexplained. Darryl was getting better at it too, he realized with regret. He braced himself as Paige opened the door.

"Yes?" she asked as she saw the agent.

"Yeah," Paige agreed. "Sorry, but I don't know much about his favorite hangouts. Did you try some of his school friends?"

"I have agents on that right now," Harkins said.

"I know his previous foster parents are out of the picture," Paige volunteered a little too willingly. "I don't think they'd have anything to do with this."

"That was one of the first things I asked about," Darryl explained. He could tell that the agent was picking up on the weird vibe between him and Paige, so he decided to back off a little and let Paige do the rest of the talking. At least that was the plan until they heard the loud crash from upstairs.

All three of them slowly looked back to the staircase as if they expected to find something come tumbling down. After a beat, Darryl found Harkins staring at the two of them with a questioning look.

"That . . . would be . . . my sisters," Paige said, obviously stalling for time.

"They're cleaning the attic," Darryl filled in the blanks. "It took them five minutes to hear me ringing the bell when I got here."

"Yeah, when we get into a project, we *really* get into a project," Paige said as another crash punctuated her statement.

Darryl wondered what was going on upstairs. He was worried on several counts: First, for to the subject of getting Harkins out of there. "Why don't we meet at the Michaels's place later. I'll call you if I find anything out in the meantime."

"Maybe I should have a look around," Harkins said.

"Oh, the place is such a mess and everything's crazy with the cleaning, as you can see," Paige said, looking down at the smashed clock on the ground. "I'd really hate for something else to nearly fall on you."

"I got it covered," Darryl added.

"If you're sure," Harkins said.

Even though Darryl nodded his consent, the agent didn't move.

"Darryl, can I see you down here for a moment?" he asked.

Darryl followed Harkins down to the sidewalk. He could see Paige stuck in the doorway, wanting to go up to help her sisters with whatever was going on, but knowing she couldn't leave just yet. He tried to hurry Harkins along by anticipating what the agent was going to say.

"I know I should have mentioned that I knew Paige and her sisters," Darryl offered. "But I was so focused on the case that I didn't realize I hadn't told you until I was halfway here."

Harkins seemed to consider Darryl's words for a moment. "Hey, I know these cases get us all a little geared up," he replied. "But we gotta keep each other in the loop on what's going on.

FBI agent wanted. For a moment, she thought back to her life before FBI agents were coming to her door . . . not to mention warlocks, and demons, and any number of other evil things. That was back when she had time in the day to work, cook for herself and her sisters, and even leave time for a bubble bath. Boy, how things had changed in recent years.

"I guess the first thing we should do is try to find out where these other Elementals are," Piper said as she crossed to the Book of Shadows.

When she reached the book, she heard Phoebe say "New plan!" and knew something was wrong. Piper turned around and saw that three rather large men and a very strong-looking woman—whom she assumed were demons— had just popped themselves inside.

Piper reflexively swung her hands up to stop time.

"There, that should—" but Piper was cut off by the fact that the demons had not frozen. The female demon then mimicked Piper's hand motion and a moment later, each of the male demons somehow managed to have a hold on Piper, Phoebe, and Leo, while the woman was grabbing for Tyler.

"What just happened?" Leo asked.

But there was no time to answer as Phoebe stomped her heel on the foot of the demon holding her and elbowed him in the gut. Then she took three giant steps across the room toward the demon's head, sending him sprawling across the floor. "But since you and Tyler are the only ones with defensive powers, I don't think we're in too much trouble."

Both women went to join Leo in fighting off the remaining two demons. Using the element of surprise, since the demons had their backs to them, Piper and Phoebe both managed to land a few good blows as Leo gave a jab to the one Phoebe attacked. These were the biggest of the demons, and they put up a good fight.

In the midst of the action, Piper saw the female demon regain consciousness and start toward Tyler again, but Piper was pinned against the wall and couldn't do anything about it.

"Phoebe!" she yelled when she saw that her sister and her husband seemed to have the other demon under control.

Phoebe moved to her sister first, but when she saw where Piper's eyes were turned, she adjusted her step toward Tyler. She grabbed Grams's mantel clock—the one she'd always hated—and threw it at the demon. The woman saw it in time to raise her arm and deflect it toward the window, where it crashed through the glass on the top.

Phoebe used the distraction to land a good blow on the woman's cheek.

She continued to the window to make sure the clock hadn't hurt anyone, since that particular window looked over the front yard, where Darryl

"Why aren't they ever 'finished'?" Phoebe asked as she checked on Tyler. "Don't they know we're the Charmed Ones? Whatever happened to giving up without a fight?"

"Pretty convenient that you just happened to have a potion nearby," Leo said. "Especially one that would kill these specific demons that we've never encountered before."

"Oh, this," Piper said. "It's a sleeping draft Paige was working on."

"So, if you threw it at the demons, what would have happened?" Tyler asked.

"Nothing much," Piper said. "Probably just leave a nasty stain."

give him a good clear spot to deposit the body. "We can hold him here and get some answers when he regains consciousness."

Darryl unceremoniously dropped the demon's feet when he reached the clearing. "You want me to interrogate him?"

"Actually, we've become surprisingly good at this," Phoebe said as she grabbed some candles off the table from which Piper had gotten the threatening sleeping potion.

"Besides, he'll know you're human . . . ," Paige said, but trailed off as if she was going to say more and chose not to.

"And therefore, not much of a threat," Darryl completed the thought. "Don't worry, I'm used to this by now."

"If it's any consolation, we might use the good cop/bad cop routine in your honor," Paige said weakly.

"Actually, I'm thinkin' just a bunch of bad cops," Phoebe said as she placed the candles in a circle around the body.

"How did things go with the FBI?" Piper asked.

"Pretty good, I think," Paige said. "The guy left."

"For the moment," Darryl added. "I think all the noise made him a little suspicious. Not to mention the fact that we wouldn't let him in the house. There's probably a car on the way with a couple of agents assigned to watch the place."

the room, never taking his eyes off the demon.

As they left the attic, Darryl realized that the demon on the floor was probably the same one that had tried to take Tyler that morning. He had thought the bruise on the demon's face had come from the fight, but realized it probably had more to do with Tyler's bat. He was even more impressed by the kid now that he knew just how big the guy was. It certainly wasn't something that he, Darryl, wanted to wake up and find hovering over him.

Darryl guided Tyler down through the house and into the living room. "Stay clear of the windows," he warned. "In case Harkins's agents return and start peeking inside. I'll go wheel the TV in from the conservatory."

"That's okay," Tyler said. "I'm not in the mood for TV."

"Things must be serious," Darryl said as he took a seat on the couch beside Tyler. "If my son ever told me he wasn't in the mood for TV I'd rush him to the hospital."

Tyler smiled, slightly. "You have a son?"

"Just a little guy," Darryl replied. "Darryl Michael Morris Junior. Once this is over, I'll have to introduce you. His mom and I are always looking for baby-sitters."

"I'm only eleven," Tyler reminded him.

"You're an eleven-year-old who can handle being chased by demons," Darryl reminded him. "It took me three years to get used to that,

"Darryl?" Tyler prodded him for an answer, rousing him from his thoughts.

"Tyler, I'm going to be honest with you," Darryl said, figuring that the kid had been through enough already in his relatively short life that he could handle the truth. "I don't know what a normal life is. I don't have any magic powers, and I'm in the middle of this just like you. What I do know is that those ladies upstairs will always be watching out for you. If they say you're going to have a normal life, then it will be as normal as they can make it for you."

"Thanks, Darryl," Tyler said, apparently satisfied with the answer.

Unfortunately, it didn't manage to ease Darryl's mind at all.

"Paige, remember how I filled the stew pot with water and left it soaking while I made the cocoa?" Piper asked as she looked over their work.

"Yeah," Paige replied.

"Would you do the honors?" Piper asked, nodding toward the unconscious demon.

"Certainly," Paige replied as she held out both hands. "Stew pot!" The pot orbed from the kitchen into her hands. She leaned the pot over the head of the demon and slowly poured out the soapy water, careful not to let it splash and put out the candles. Once a third of the water had been poured on his head, the demon woke, spitting soap from his mouth.

"Phoebe, the spell," Piper said, holding out her hand to her sister.

"Okay, I'll tell you," the demon replied rather easily.

Piper knew that was the benefit of dealing with minions. They very rarely had loyalty to their masters when faced with imminent death, and could always be counted on to squeal like demonic pigs.

"We went after the kid after we lost the first Firestarter," the demon said.

"The guy that jumped off the Golden Gate?" Phoebe asked for clarification.

The demon nodded his head. "He didn't know that we knew where he lived . . . well, *when* he lived, that is." He laughed at his own little joke. "He did a bunch of research finding the other Elementals, including the kid. Apparently, he wanted to have a backup in case something happened to him. Good planning, eh?"

He waited for a response, but there was none.

"Was really organized too," the minion continued. "Told us everything we needed to know about the other three Elementals and the little Firestarter."

"Except that Tyler's powers were bound," Piper said, mentally confirming what they had already suspected about there being three other Elementals.

"Yeah, he left that part out," the demon replied. "But I found that out this morning when afternoon if they let him. "And neither do we. . . . Phoebe."

Phoebe held out the paper as she, Piper, and Paige read aloud:

> *This one's going down*
> *Only three more to go.*
> *Then Tempest will frown,*
> *As we vanquish our foe.*

The demon let out a horrible scream that echoed through the house as he exploded in a colorful light show. Conveniently, the window was already open—and smashed, too—so the smoke from the burning demon blew away quickly.

"Then Tempest will frown?" Paige asked, skeptically.

"Hey, it was all I could come up with on short notice," Phoebe replied. "I said it wasn't my best work."

Piper watched the last of the demon smoke fly out the window and noticed that it was beginning to rain. "We should cover that or something, before all the rain comes in."

"I'll take care of it," Leo said. He was used to making quick patches around the house, what with the tendency of uninvited guests toward smashing the place up. "But first, how are we going to find the rest of the Elementals?"

"I have an idea about that," Piper replied. "Meet us downstairs when you're done."

need anyone else to come poking around.

"Maybe we can go back upstairs now," Tyler suggested.

"That's okay," Piper said. "We thought we'd bring the party to you."

The Charmed Ones filled Darryl and Tyler in on what little they had learned upstairs. It only took a moment, and had Darryl worrying once again what their next move would be.

"So, what's the plan?" he asked. "How do we find the Elementals?"

"Tyler," Piper said. "Did I ever tell you about scrying?"

"Is that where you use the crystal and the map to find someone?" Tyler asked. "Paige showed me how when Britney Spears was in town."

All the adults in the room shot Paige a look.

"What? He's a preteen boy, who else would he want to locate?" she said, defending her actions and choice of person to scry.

"Don't you need a personal object or something to do that?" Darryl asked. He had watched the Charmed Ones scry on occasion.

"He had her CD," Paige said. "It was good enough."

"No, I meant with the Elementals," Darryl said with a laugh.

"Oh," Paige simply replied.

"I was thinking that Tyler must have a connection to the other Elementals," Piper said. "We

"Did I do it right?" Tyler asked, looking over his shoulder at Paige.

"Well, sort of," Paige replied as she leaned down over the map. "You found yourself."

Since Darryl was the closest to the map, he leaned in and saw that the scrying crystal had, in fact, landed directly on Halliwell Manor. "It's a start," he said encouragingly. "Now just find the other three."

Darryl could see a look of frustration briefly cross Tyler's face, but he had to give the kid props for pulling the chain back up and swinging it over the map once again without a grumble or a complaint. It was bad enough that Darryl had to deal with all this crazy magic stuff as an adult; he couldn't imagine going through it all at Tyler's age.

It took a few minutes, but Tyler and Paige managed to drop the scrying crystal on three more points on the map of San Francisco. Naturally, the other three Elementals had to currently be spread across the city.

The first drop of the scrying crystal—after it had located Tyler—landed on a building in the financial district. Considering that it was already Saturday afternoon, Darryl figured that there would be less people in that area to get in the way, which was lucky. The second location appeared to be an elementary school in Stonestown, though Darryl couldn't imagine who would be in a school on Saturday other

That response was met by silence. It was obvious that Leo and the Charmed Ones were reluctant to bring that kind of threat straight to Darryl's family, but he knew that there was no other option.

"Little Darryl is with his grandparents for the night," Darryl explained. "So only Sheila's at the house. If those demons only found Tyler here because your address was in some guy's notes, then the odds of them finding my place are slim."

"But what if they're watching the Manor right now?" Paige asked. "They could follow you home and attack."

"I've followed enough people in my life to know how to lose a tail," Darryl said. "Besides, there'd be no reason to follow me, since I won't be seen leaving the house with Tyler."

"You'll need me to orb him to your place," Leo said, catching on.

"Actually, I need you to do something else," Piper said. "Paige will have to do the orbing."

"Fine with me," Paige said as she gave Tyler a smile. "And maybe we can stop off on the way and pick up some clothes for you. Unless you're okay with being in your pajamas all day?"

"Clothes would be nice," Tyler agreed.

"Just be careful," Phoebe warned. "His picture's probably all over the place by now."

"I am nothing if not the queen of stealth," Paige replied.

like we're all leaving at once. The agents will probably keep watching the house, especially if they think Paige is still inside."

"You don't think they might come to the door?" Paige asked.

"Well, they don't know that you didn't already leave before they got here," Darryl said. "When you and Tyler orb over, meet me in the garage. I think Sheila will have fewer questions if I come in with him instead of you bringing him to me."

"Got it," Paige said, giving a little mock salute.

Tyler, however, looked a little tentative about leaving the Charmed Ones.

"Hey, Tyler," Darryl said. "You'll like it at my place. I've got Gamecube and a ton of games."

"Do you have SSX3?" Tyler asked, his eyes practically bugging out.

Darryl smiled and nodded.

Suddenly, Tyler looked quite eager to get there.

Darryl wished the ladies and Leo luck and made his way out of the house after promising to keep his cell phone open should they need him and Tyler to get somewhere on a moment's notice. As he stepped out into the rain, he did another quick check up and down the block, but only saw the agents' car. He gave them a little wave as he got into his own car and wasn't surprised when they waved back, confirming that

Darryl carefully pocketed the potion, not wanting to risk breaking the one magical defense he had against attack. Once he was sure it was safe, he turned his attention to Tyler, who looked much calmer than he had at the Manor. "Hey, Tyler, nice threads."

"Thanks," Tyler replied. He looked like he'd stepped straight out of a Gap Kids ad.

"I don't think we've really thanked you for this," Paige said.

She was about to say more, but Darryl silenced her by raising his hand. He looked down at Tyler, who epitomized the word "innocence."

"Just doing my job," Darryl said.

"I take it that opportunity never arose?" he asked.

The female seemed reluctant to speak. She looked back to the others, but they provided no support whatsoever.

"We saw a man and two of the witches leave the house," she explained. "We thought that left only two adults with the Firestarter."

"And?"

"When we were teleported back inside, the house was empty," she continued, hardly masking the confusion in her voice. "We searched from top to bottom, but it was like they disappeared."

"Maybe because they did," Tempest suggested.

"Yes, master," she said. "We humbly apologize."

"Stop!" Tempest said as the three minions started to bow. "We're wasting time. Move on to the next phase of the plan. Once you collect the powers from the other Elementals you can go back for the Firestarter."

"Yes, master," the female said as she and the big guys looked up at their leader in awe of his plan.

"Well . . . go."

Once Paige had turned Tyler over to Darryl, she orbed to the Stonestown section of San Francisco and right into the auditorium of Woodrow never have this kind of education simply because of the part of the city their parents had chosen to live in. Okay, she knew that she was jumping to conclusions without really knowing the school, but when she peeked into the room full of brand new Apple G4 computers, it sent her head spinning.

She was considering orbing into the locked room to check things out when the sound of a crash from down the hall reminded her why she was at the school in the first place. Paige took off down the hall, but was careful not to run directly into the commotion. Her caution was rewarded when a chair came flying out of a classroom and just missed her head. If she had been only one step ahead of herself, she would probably be unconscious on the cold, yet sparkling clean, floor.

Paige exercised even more caution as she peeked into the classroom and took in the situation.

The place was unlike any classroom that she had had in her childhood. First of all, there were no desks on the carpeted floor. There were a few chairs and a stack of mats along the multicolored wall. The only desk in the room was the teacher's, and that looked more like it was from Ikea than from any warehouse that specialized in those big, wooden school desks that looked like they weighed a thousand pounds. This desk seemed rather flimsy by comparison—a fact that

"Long story," she replied. "We have to get you out of here."

"I've got to get these animals out of here," he said.

"Animals?" Paige asked. For the first time she noticed that the far wall was lined with cages and terrariums filled with small critters ranging from iguanas to what looked to be possums. She did appreciate the guy's concern for the critters, but they weren't the ones in danger. "What kind of class *is* this?"

Paige didn't have time to find out the answer to her question because the demon had managed to extricate himself entirely from the pile and was moving toward them menacingly.

"We can come back for the animals," Paige said. "But we should get someplace safer."

"I'll create a diversion," Rafe said as he shut his eyes to concentrate.

"Wait," she warned, but once again it was too late. Paige watched as the demon was pelted by chalk.

"Run!" Rafe said as he dashed out from behind the desk and past the demon.

Paige had no choice but to follow. She hunched down, bracing herself for the demon's counterattack, but none came.

"This way," Rafe said once they were out in the hall. He ran in the direction that Paige had come, back to the auditorium. "Now can you tell me who's after me . . . and why?"

"Fat chance," Paige said as they darted across the stage. "What happened before I got here? And what are you doing in school on a Saturday?"

"One of my student's parents works at the zoo," Rafe explained as he led Paige through the backstage area, past smaller classrooms and storage areas. "She lent us all the animals you saw in my room for the week. I came in to pick up the cages and return them to the zoo. Had to wait for the weekend so I could borrow my friend's truck."

"And that's when the demon attacked?" Paige asked.

"You keep saying demon," Rafe said, incredulous about the information. "What? Like Satan's minion or something?"

"Minion, yes. Satan, not so much," Paige said, trying to keep the conversation on track. She didn't blame him for the confusion. It was a lot to take in. "Anyway, did he use some kind of power on you?"

"No," Rafe said. "He just threatened me with his big bulky body. I considered fighting him off, but did you see the size of his arms?"

"Yeah," Paige said. The guy was impressive, but she knew her sisters had already taken the demon on once that day. She chose to leave that part out, in deference to the feelings of the guy she was trying to save.

"At first I thought he was a mugger," he said.

hand and a sky blue energy flowed out of Rafe's body toward the demon. She saw Rafe's mask of concentration break and turn into a look of shock.

The demon was draining his power.

"Here's a little snack," Sheila Morris said as she put a bowl of microwave macaroni and cheese along with a juice box in front of Tyler, who was sitting at the kitchen table. "Enjoy. Darryl and I will be out in the living room if you need us."

Darryl knew he was in for it. He had only given Sheila a brief—and carefully high-lighted—explanation of the chain of events that led him to secretly bring a missing child into their home. He knew that Sheila wouldn't cause a problem in front the boy, but now that she had gotten him out of the way with a quick meal, Darryl knew he was in for it.

"Now, let me explain before you go off on me," Darryl said with a lighthearted smile as his wife joined him in the living room.

"Don't you smile at me," Sheila said, calmly. "Who are these people looking for Tyler?"

"It has to do with his past," Darryl said, choosing his words carefully. He had no problem *concealing* the truth from her, but it was the outright lying that he wasn't comfortable doing. "Before he was adopted."

"So, what? Evil foster parents?" Sheila asked.

"Something like that," Darryl agreed, going

"You bringing him home with you," Sheila replied.

"You're the only one who can bring work home?" Darryl asked, making a lame attempt at a joke.

Sheila only smiled slightly as she shook her head in resignation. "I don't suppose the Halliwells are involved in this somehow."

It was all Darryl could do to maintain his neutral expression and not reveal his shock. Sheila was much more in tune to events than he had suspected. It shouldn't have surprised him. She was an amazing woman.

"Darryl, if I go in there and ask Tyler if he knows Piper, Phoebe, and Paige, what will he say?" Sheila asked, getting up from the couch and approaching her husband.

"That you are one good detective," Darryl replied.

"Don't try to butter me up," Sheila said. "Tell me what's going on."

"I would, honey," Darryl said. "But it's not my secret to tell. And right now I need to focus on keeping that boy safe. Can we please leave this discussion for some other time?"

"Okay," Sheila agreed. "But don't you think I'm going to forget about this."

"I love you," Darryl said.

"You'd better," Sheila replied with a laugh as they kissed.

Their brief moment of romance was interrupted when Darryl's cell phone rang. He took

"Your boss doesn't even know that you found the kid?" Sheila asked.

"Look, it's complicated," Darryl said. "I can't get too many people involved.

"At least tell me his parents know that their son is being protected," she said.

Darryl's silence gave her the answer.

"Those people are probably worried sick," Sheila said. "How can you have their child here and let them worry like that?"

"I said it was complicated," he replied, trying to figure out how much of the story he could share.

"That is not acceptable," Sheila said. "You get back there and tell them their son is safe. I'll watch Tyler."

At that moment Tyler just happened into the room. "Are you going somewhere?" he asked, the concern showing in his voice.

"Darryl's going to let your parent's know you're okay," Sheila said as she moved over to the boy and put a calming hand on his shoulder. "He won't be gone long."

Darryl knew that he really didn't have a choice in the matter. Aside from the fact that his wife was putting her foot down, he didn't want to put his job in jeopardy either. Besides, an appearance at the crime scene would go a long way toward making his actions look less suspicious. Naturally, he had to weigh all those facts against leaving his wife unprotected and

"Be careful," Sheila said as she gave him a kiss on the cheek.

"Don't open the door for anyone you don't know," Darryl said, doubting that demons would use the door to get in. "And if someone gets in the house, don't try to be a hero. Just grab Tyler and go."

"I love you," she said as she pushed him to the door.

"I love you too," he replied, worrying that he was making a huge mistake.

Phoebe considered asking for help at the information desk but she worried that she'd be sent to the psych ward if she asked if they knew if anyone with the power to control the elements was on the premises.

Phoebe bypassed the lobby, heading down a long hall to her right toward the emergency room. She figured that was as good a place as any to start, and an even better place to wind up should one of Tempest's demons attack. The problem was, she still didn't have an idea how she was going to locate the Elemental.

She briefly considered touching everyone she passed, hoping that one of them showed her a future with Tyler in it. But that plan had several flaws. First of all, she couldn't just go around touching every single person in the hospital. Then there was the possible problem of seeing other people's futures that could distract her from her mission. On top of that, a hospital was not exactly the kind of place where you want to go touching potentially germ-filled people.

As she reached the ER, Phoebe passed a large tropical fish tank set into the wall. The search narrowed when she saw the water in the tank swirling in a violent whirlpool, sending the fish in circles at dizzying speeds. Phoebe looked through the water and saw a slightly frazzled African-American woman in a lab coat flipping through some charts.

"Bingo!" Phoebe said as she walked to the

"Gabrielle," the med student replied. "Gabrielle Chambers. What do you mean, save the world?"

"Let's start at the beginning," Phoebe said, taking a seat. "How long have you been able to control water?"

"Control water?" the woman said, sitting beside her. "I don't know what you're talking about."

"Look I—we—don't have time for games," Phoebe said.

"No, honestly," Gabrielle said. "I really *don't* know what you're talking about. All my life I've been comfortable around the water. I love to swim and surf and go boating. And yeah, every now and then I notice weird things happening, like the water in the tank just now. But I'm not *controlling* it."

Phoebe didn't know where to begin. It was one thing to tell the woman she had to use her power to save the world, it was quite another to have to start from scratch and tell her that she had a power that she could use to save the world.

"Although that does explain that time I walked on water," Gabrielle said. "I just thought I was on a sandbar out in the ocean. Now you're telling me that I did that? I can make the water do what I want . . . like Aquaman?"

"Actually, I think he just tells the fish what to do," Phoebe replied. "But yeah, you can make water do what you want it to do."

"Wow," Gabrielle said.

Phoebe looked through the broken glass to see one of the demons standing in the hall.

Piper reached the glass doors of the bank and pulled, knowing that they would be locked. She was right. The sign on the door indicated that the bank had closed an hour earlier.

"Stupid Saturday hours," she mumbled to herself as she tried to stay dry under the small overhang. The rain was coming down harder, and the sky was so dark it almost appeared as if it was already night.

Piper banged against the glass door, worried that her Elemental may have left. She peered inside, but the place looked entirely empty.

"Hello!" she called out as she banged on the glass once again. "Is anybody in there?"

This time, her knocking was rewarded when she saw an older woman come out of an office in the back. She looked to be in her mid-sixties and was dressed in a very professional dark blue suit.

It took the woman almost a minute to get across the huge bank lobby, during which time Piper got more and more soaked by the rain. She used the delay to test her speech out in her mind. She thought, for some reason, it might be difficult to convince the woman that she had to come along with her to stop a demon from controlling the weather and taking over the world. Although Piper was getting more and more used to telling people weird magical truths.

Chapter

10

"Paige . . . help . . . ," Rafe said in a strained voice as his power continued to be drained from his body.

Paige wondered why the demon hadn't drained Rafe's power when he'd used it earlier. She didn't have much time to think it over as Rafe's knees buckled and he fell to the ground. Luckily, she came up with a possible solution rather quickly. She figured it was safe to orb so she popped herself behind the demon and kicked him in the weak spot in the back of his knees.

The demon stumbled and broke his hold on Rafe, which snapped the blue light in two. Rafe looked a little weak, but he was able to stand.

"Try to use your power on the computers," she said, pointing to the cabinet over the demon.

Rafe got the idea and focused on the shelves.

endless school, "you're what's known as an Elemental."

"Okay," Rafe said, absorbing her words. "So, what's the difference between being telekinetic and being an . . ."

"Elemental."

"Yeah . . . that."

They burst through a set of wooden doors, and Paige was surprised to find that they were in the school gym. At first she wondered why he had taken her to the big room with nothing to hide behind, but then she saw the equipment locker. It was already standing open and littered with possible weapons. Images of past dodge-ball games came to mind, and she and Rafe ran to the locker to prepare for battle.

"Telekinesis is a whole mind-over-matter thing," Paige explained as they pulled every-thing out of the locker. "What *you* do is use your emotions to control the winds to lift and move things. You're not moving the objects so much as letting them ride the wind currents you create."

"Really?" Rafe said, sounding impressed with himself. "So I could, like, fly if I wanted to?"

"Yep. You, like, could do that," she replied, making fun of the teacher.

Paige was just one flip of the hair away from flirting with the guy, but she realized that and stopped herself. She hadn't had the best luck with men lately, particularly ones that got involved in her magical life. She decided to there were also several news vans littering the street. The case had somehow gone from simple kidnapping to full media event.

Just what we need, Darryl thought.

Various members of the media were camped in the middle of the street interviewing neighbors and the dozens of people who just came by to witness real news in the making. They all seemed unfazed by the heavy rainfall pelting them, not wanting to miss out on their chance to be part of the story.

Uniformed officers had taped off the area to keep the people back. Darryl would have had to show ID just to get his car on the street, but the officer recognized him and waved him through. It had not looked like this at all when Darryl had left, and that was probably why the chief had called him and politely pointed out that he really needed to be there.

Darryl was always amazed by the public's interest in certain missing child cases. He knew for a fact that kids went missing every day across the U.S., but rarely did they warrant such media attention. Once Darryl thought about it, though, he wasn't really surprised. Tyler's case had the markings of one of those media blitzes—recently adopted Caucasian child in a semi-affluent neighborhood goes missing in the early morning . . . a bloody bat found at the scene. Granted, Darryl knew there was only a *trace* amount of blood on the bat, but by the time it what sounded like relief in her voice as she called Darryl into the living room. "We were wondering what happened to you."

"Call me Darryl," he reminded them as he joined them. "I'm sorry, but I had to check up on a few things. I hope Agent Harkins has been okay with you."

"He's got so many people around him, it's hard to get a word in," Mr. Michaels replied after he took the cigarette out of his mouth. "Not that we're complaining. The more people working on the case, the better."

"We were wondering if they could issue one of those Amber Alerts?" Maria asked with hope in her voice and her eyes.

Darryl hated to be the one to dash that hope. "We can only do that if there's information on a vehicle that may have been involved. I saw Agent Harkins working to spread the word through the press when I came in. That will help almost as much as a formal alert."

"We just want to try everything," Stephen said as he kept holding on to his unlit cigarette.

Darryl's heart was breaking watching the couple and knowing that their son was probably playing video games with Sheila right now. His wife always acted like the games were a waste of time and brain cells, but Darryl had caught her quickly switching off the Gamecube on a couple of occasions when he came home early from work.

parents?" Stephen asked. "The ones who went missing?"

"In a way," Darryl went with the lie they provided just as he had done earlier with Sheila. "It's a difficult situation to explain. Things are changing by the minute. But I wanted you to know that Paige Matthews is involved and taking care of it." He hadn't wanted to mention Paige by name, but figured it was a little something to give the couple so they would, hopefully, refrain from asking too many questions.

"That's wonderful," Maria practically screamed. "When can we see him?"

Stephen, however, was slightly more reserved. "Darryl, why couldn't you tell us this in the living room? What's going on?"

Darryl knew that was a question he couldn't even attempt to answer. "The next few hours are going to be critical," he said.

"Critical? What do you mean?" Maria asked. "Do you have our son or not?"

"I know where he is," Darryl said. "But I'd be lying if I didn't tell you his life could still be in danger."

"Oh, God," Maria said as she dropped into an armchair.

"Like I said, we've got people working on it," Darryl said, trying to sound positive. "But I need you both to do something for me."

"What? Anything," Maria said, and her husband shook his head in agreement.

of their trust bear down on him even more.

He was making his way out of the house when he met face to face with Agent Harkins.

"Darryl," the agent said genially. "I was wondering what happened to you. Any luck with the social worker?"

"Nothing solid," Darryl replied. "How are things here?"

"We're doing the best we can with what little we've got," Harkins replied. "Do you think you can get me a formal report on Paige Matthews and her sisters?"

"Sure," Darryl said, though he wondered what Harkins was getting at. They had worked so well together in the past largely because when Darryl told the guy they'd hit a dead end, Harkins took him at face value, without question. "I was planning on heading back to the station." That was a complete lie, but he figured it was better than telling Harkins where he was really going.

"Great," Harkins said as he made a little notation on his notepad. "Still wish you would've told me you were going over there."

"Yeah," Darryl replied. "Sorry about that."

"No, it's okay." Harkins said as he slid the notepad into his pocket. "It seems to have worked itself out. I just didn't realize how close you were to the family."

"What do you mean?" Darryl asked with concern over the direction this conversation was going.

Chapter

11

"Get down!" Phoebe yelled as she knocked Gabrielle to the ground just in time to avoid the fire extinguisher the demon had flung at the woman. It was cold and wet on the linoleum, and tropical fish were flopping on the floor around them.

The demon leaped though the now empty hole in the wall and moved toward Gabrielle with his hands reaching out, ready to lay them on her to drain the power she'd just learned that she had.

Phoebe hopped back up and let her magic carry her higher as she let loose with a barrage of kicks at the demon that sent his back to the wall. As she descended, she noticed that the crash had alerted numerous people to the situation, which meant she would have to stay earthbound for the moment or risk exposing her secret.

"Call security," someone said rather calmly,

A crowd was gathering in the hall, though none of those people seemed as heroic as the two guys that had just gotten themselves thrown aside. Or maybe that was the reason the rest of the group chose to remain passive observers.

How long does it take security to get here? Phoebe wondered as she considered her options. Even when the guards showed up, she figured they wouldn't be armed. They'd probably be sweet old retired cops that didn't have a chance against tall, dark, and gruesome.

That made the decision for her, and she ran to the vending machine without hesitation. The demon moved a half-second after she did, bending low so he could get the glass shard first.

Since the room wasn't that large, it was only a few steps before Phoebe and demon were about to collide. Phoebe used the momentum from the demon's considerable bulk against him as she shifted her plan mid-stride.

The floor by the vending machine was wet, so as the demon bent he also slid into the machine. Phoebe reached behind the machine and pulled from the top, using all her strength to bring it down on the demon, trapping him on the floor.

Luckily, the machine stayed in one piece and didn't smash on the wet floor, electrocuting them all. Phoebe only realized that potential flaw in her plan after it didn't happen.

The crowd cheered as an ER doctor came in and sedated the struggling demon. Security

The med student looked up at her like she was crazy. "Demon? You just stopped a demon from . . . what? Killing me?"

"Kidnapping," Phoebe said. "And I didn't stop him so much as slow him down."

"The cops are going to take him away," Gabrielle said. "As far as I'm concerned, it's over."

"Oh, but it's *so* not," Phoebe said as she calmly tried to explain just how *not* over this day was for Gabrielle.

The med student seemed to take everything in stride. She listened politely and didn't interrupt with any questions. Phoebe was quite hopeful by the end of her little speech, in spite of the dramatic pause Gabrielle took before she spoke.

Phoebe understood Gabrielle's hesitation. Being charged with saving the world was a lot to take in, especially in the middle of the workday. But once she accepted the fact that she had an even greater mission in life than just being a doctor, Phoebe knew that they would be on their way home and to the next stage of their plan.

"I'm sorry," Gabrielle said. "But I'm not going anywhere."

Piper sipped at the hot cup of coffee the woman had made for her to combat the chill from the rain. She took Piper back to her office, introduced herself as Muriel Hammond, and explained that she was alone in the place after hours because she was the bank president. However, she still

"It can be," Muriel said. "I've done a tremendous amount of research on it over the course of my life. It can literally shape the world, if put to good use. And don't you think it isn't very tempting to know you have the power to destroy anyone that gets in your way."

Don't I know it, Piper thought.

"But I never abuse the power," Muriel quickly added. "Well, okay . . . once. But that woman at the country club was just so annoying. She really needed a dip in the pool to cool off. I just helped by having the ground give her a little push."

Piper laughed. She wasn't allowed to use her powers for any kind of personal gain—not even by punishing a man who refused to pick up after his dog. She and her sisters had been finding ways to bend that little rule recently, but they always had to be careful not to cross the line. Even so, it was nice to meet someone with a power she could exploit if she wanted to, but still chose not to of her own free will.

"How long have you known you were an Earthshaker?" Piper asked. She and Phoebe had found out they were witches only after their Grams died when they were adults. Paige was grown when she learned about herself as well.

"All my life," Muriel replied. "I know the books say that Elementals are rare, but what's even more rare is that the Earthshaker ability seems to run in my family. We've had the power was the Firestarter originally charged with the responsibility of gathering the Elementals, but he didn't have the chance to fulfill his task."

"The Firestarter who jumped off the Golden Gate," Piper guessed.

Muriel nodded her head sadly. "Christopher . . . I wish I had been here when he sent the file."

Piper looked at her, questioningly.

"I was in Los Angeles for the week," Muriel explained as she sat and took a drink of her coffee. "I just got back in town this morning. My desk was so laden with work that it took me a half hour to notice the file in my inbox. By then I had heard reports of the missing boy. I figured if he had been taken, Tempest would have come after me already."

"You know about Tempest?" Piper asked.

"Like I said, this power's been in my family for generations," Muriel continued. "My ancestors dealt with the demon before, though I've certainly never met him in person. I may be old, but the last time he was out and about was a hundred years ago."

"But you knew Tyler was on the run," Piper tried to clarify, wondering why the woman didn't make her presence known earlier.

"And I suspected he would run to the safety of the Charmed Ones," Muriel explained. "When we get close to the Night of Aeolus, it is the Firestarter who becomes the most open target for Tempest's demons. Since he or she is charged

"So you found them already," Muriel said, returning to her warm smile. "I knew the reputation of the Charmed Ones wasn't an exaggeration. But your sisters could be in for a difficult time. The Windwalker and Waterbearer have no idea about any of this."

"If Christopher contacted you, why didn't he tell the others?" Piper asked.

"Oh, he didn't contact me," Muriel said. "I found him."

Piper tried to wrap her mind around this very involved set of circumstances.

"The Firestarter usually waits until that last moment to alert the other Elementals," Muriel continued her explanation. "So they can remain safe. While he waited, Christopher tried to find out all the information that he could about each of us so he would know the best way to approach us with the news. As I said before, if you spend your life not knowing who you really are, it can be a bit of a shock to find out."

"Tell me about it," Piper mumbled.

"Since I knew the Night was coming, it wasn't hard to figure out I was being watched," Muriel said. "So I met up with Christopher and told him he could stop following me. He was relieved that I was one less thing for him to worry about, especially since he had found out I was going out of town for the week leading up to the ritual. Besides, I know how to protect myself from demons."

Chapter

12

Paige and Rafe each grabbed one of the demon's legs and dragged his unconscious body across the highly polished gym floor to the equipment locker—or "weapons locker" as Paige had christened it in her mind. The barrage of footballs, basketballs, and field hockey sticks they had let loose on the demon had been quite effective at knocking him cold.

"So this Ritual of the Guardians thing," Rafe said, still working out what Paige had told him after the battle. "What do I have to do exactly?"

"Exactly?" Paige asked, grasping for an explanation. "Well, we don't know . . . exactly. But it's very important." Somehow, this all sounded so much more convincing in her head.

"Oh, I get that part," Rafe said as they unceremoniously dumped the demon in the equipment on my power to control the wind and all that 'saving the world' stuff without overwhelming me with it," he said. "Especially considering you hit some of the high points while battling a demon. It made me think you'd do pretty well against a class of fourth graders."

"Demons . . . kids . . . it's all the same to me," Paige said with a laugh as she reached into her pocket and pulled out a potion. "Certainly gives me something else to think about."

"Got a lot on your mind?" Rafe asked.

"I've been in a bit of a rut lately," she said as she uncorked the bottle of green liquid. "Sleeping potion," she explained before Rafe asked the question. "I figure we can keep him knocked out here for a while, then come back after I have time to make a proper vanquishing potion . . . or bring my sister. She's good at blowing things up."

"You have a sister?" Rafe asked, feigning interest.

"Back off, she's married," Paige replied. "Although I do have another sister. But she's a little . . . emotionally unavailable at the moment."

"Bad breakup?" he asked, prying slightly.

"Divorced a demon," Paige nodded as she poured the potion down the unconscious guy's throat. "You know, they're kinda cute when they're sleeping," she kidded.

The demon choked a little on the mixture, but didn't wake.

"No one else should be in the building until Monday," Rafe said. "We just have to be sure to

"Like I said at the Manor," Darryl finally replied before Harkins could ask again, "Paige Matthews was a dead end. She really couldn't tell me anything more than Mr. and Mrs. Michaels had."

"I never understood why people got so pretentious with houses," Harkins said. "True, the place looked big—at least from the outside—but to call it a 'manor' just seems a little arrogant, don't you think?"

"It's a family thing," Darryl said, immediately knowing that he'd chosen the wrong answer.

"So, you know the family pretty well then?" Harkins asked.

"Their sister used to be involved with my partner," Darryl said.

"Yeah," Harkins said, genuinely saddened by the mention. "Andy was a good guy. Didn't the sister die too?"

Darryl didn't want to dwell in the past, especially considering it was such a sad subject. "The family has had its fair share of tragedy," he admitted. "I don't see what that has to do with the case we're working on. They're not even involved."

That was probably the biggest lie Darryl had told all day.

"Well, they might not be directly," Harkins said, trying to keep his voice low. "But they are at the very least peripherally involved with the case and numerous others that you've investigated."

"You've earned that level of trust from me. But I'm talking big picture here, Darryl. If you keep getting involved in these weird cases with missing suspects and these girls . . . I'm just concerned for your future."

"I appreciate that," Darryl said, and he meant it. "But everything's under control. I promise you."

"All right, then." Harkins dropped the subject. "We've got a missing child to find."

"I'm on it," Darryl said, mustering up false enthusiasm as he moved toward the door. He took one last glance toward Stephen and Maria who were back on their couch trying not to look too comforted by what Darryl had told them. Maria was even back to mangling the throw pillow, though Darryl assumed that had more to do with actual concern for Tyler than covering for Darryl. He knew he'd just taken a great risk by letting them know that their son was possibly okay. Aside from the fact that it was premature, it was certainly dangerous in light of Harkins's words.

"Keep me posted," Harkins called to him.

"You know it," Darryl lied as he stepped back out into the storm.

It was raining even harder than it had been when Darryl had entered the house. The wind had kicked up as well and was blowing the tent around the yard. Several agents were trying to grab the canvas and put the thing away. Darryl hoped they would hurry because the sky was filling with lightning and they really have to distance himself from the Charmed Ones for their own safety.

Then again, that might not be such a bad idea, he thought.

Because he was in a moving car, Darryl didn't notice the slight rumble beneath his tires. But he couldn't miss it when the road started to buckle in front of him.

The trees along the sides of the road swayed as the earthquake hit full force.

Darryl resisted the temptation to slam on his brakes and tried to roll to a stop, but the ground had different plans. A rough jolt forced his foot to slip from the brake pedal to the gas. The short burst of speed sent his car careening out of control on the rain-slicked street.

As he rushed toward a building, Darryl panicked and slammed on the brakes, overcompensating for his original slip and sending the car fishtailing and ultimately spinning in a total loss of control. The car hopped a curb and slammed sideways into the building.

Darryl blacked out for a second, but managed to rouse himself. His entire body ached. When his eyes fluttered open he noticed that the side impact airbag had deflated, and his seatbelt had locked him in place. He could feel the rain spattering on his face. The front windshield was totally gone.

The water wasn't the concern though; it was the piece of metal sticking out of his chest that worried him as he blacked out for good.

Piper leaned back on the desk as she tried to come up with some other, less deadly, options. Her hand brushed against the cup of hot coffee and she was immediately glad that she hadn't drunk the whole thing. Now she just needed a distraction.

Her wish was granted as the ground beneath her started to rumble. A distraction was on the way, but it wasn't the kind that she wanted.

The demon obviously noticed the slight rumble as the evil smile on her face widened considerably. "That's right, Earthshaker. Use your power against me."

"Muriel," Piper warned, without looking back.

"Hey, that's not me," Muriel replied. "I think you should brace—"

But she wasn't able to get the full warning out as the earthquake hit, sending all three women stumbling to keep their balance. Books fell off the shelves to Piper's right and the computer crashed to the floor behind her. It was the distraction she was hoping for . . . and then some.

Piper grabbed the coffee and threw it in the demon's face as she tried to get her footing. The woman screamed and dropped the gun.

"Run!" Piper said as she reached back and took Muriel's hand, pulling her out the door of her office. She considered going for the gun, but a pile of books landed on top of it after sliding off the desk.

someone to fix the door. I'm going home to check on my place."

She hung up the phone before the person on the other end could respond.

Piper looked at her in amazement as they reached the SUV.

"Bank manager," Muriel explained. "Can't let a little demon get in the way of my investment."

Piper continued to admire the woman's abilities as she belted in and started the SUV, pulling out of the spot without looking. Through the intense rain, she could see a shape approaching them. A bolt of lightning lit the sky and revealed that it was the demon, with her gun aimed at them.

"Floor it!" Muriel said as she put on her seatbelt and held on to the dash.

Piper did as instructed and slammed the pedal. The SUV's tires screeched as they found traction on the wet ground.

The demon managed to fire one off as the SUV bore down on her. She was aiming at Piper, but the shot went wide and merely nicked the side view mirror.

"Hold on!" Piper yelled as they were about to hit.

The demon was about to fire off another round when she realized that her life was in very real danger. Choosing to live and fight another day, she popped herself out of there using the demon equivalent of orbing.

on the other side of the door, buckling those lockers in the middle. Phoebe tried to see if she could fit under the lockers, but realized that she wasn't going to get very far since the door opened *into* the room.

"Give me a hand?" Phoebe asked, suspecting that any effort would be futile.

Gabrielle joined Phoebe at the lockers. They both put a shoulder against the metal and tried to push it up and out of the way. The lockers slid about a half-inch before getting stuck.

"Okay," Phoebe said, straining against the metal. "I don't think this is working."

They took a step back to examine the situation further.

"Can't you just levitate the lockers?" Gabrielle asked. "Like you did when that guy attacked."

"That levitation thing only works on me," Phoebe said. "It's not exactly the most useful power, to be honest. It certainly won't help us here. We might be stuck until someone comes for us."

"We're in a hospital following a fairly decent quake," Gabrielle said. "Everybody's going to be too busy to come looking for us for a while."

Phoebe looked around the room, trying to find something to leverage against the lockers. The broken bed frame was looking like their best shot, when Phoebe saw something else that gave her an idea. "Maybe we can use some water pressure."

"You've got to be kidding," Gabrielle said as

Nothing happened.

"Don't think," Phoebe said, realizing that she was talking to a former lawyer who was now a medical student. The odds that Gabrielle could stop thinking were slim to say the least. "You just have to feel the water. Let it touch your emotions."

Phoebe didn't have a clue what she was talking about, but it seemed to be working. The puddle of water stopped spreading across the room and focused itself under the lockers.

Gabrielle had closed her eyes, so she didn't know the progress she was making.

"You're doing it," Phoebe said as more water was pulled out of the pipes.

"I'm doing it?" Gabrielle asked as her eyes popped open. "I'm doing it!"

Phoebe figured that Gabrielle's excitement level must have affected her control, because the water suddenly shot up at the lockers, blowing them back against the wall. Both Phoebe and Gabrielle jumped as the water came crashing down on them, giving them each a good soaking.

"That was great," Phoebe said, putting her hand on Gabrielle's soggy back.

"Wow," was all Gabrielle could say.

Phoebe gave the woman a moment to absorb what had happened, but it was a quick moment.

"Now," Phoebe said, "I need you and your power to come with me."

behind the curtained-off section of the ER. Phoebe considered following the woman behind the curtain, but the pained moaning coming from the other side told her it wasn't the best course of action.

The general chaos of the ER was increasing and Phoebe knew that she wasn't going to convince Gabrielle to leave with her. She could only hope that things would be a little calmer in a few hours.

Phoebe decided to head back to her car and find out how the others had done on their respective assignments. She tried using her cell phone to reach her sisters, but she only got a message that said NO SERVICE.

The rain was really coming down and the sounds of sirens echoed in every direction as she pulled out of the parking garage. Phoebe had to slam on the brakes to avoid hitting an ambulance rushing past her.

Once she determined the coast was clear, Phoebe carefully took to the street, unaware that the ambulance that just passed was carrying her badly injured friend, Darryl.

"I can find them," she said. "I can still feel them. Let me go to the hospital . . . to the school."

"No," Tempest said. "I need at least one of you to remain alive until tonight. Well, it's not a total necessity, but it would certainly make *my* life easier. What say you work with me here? Haven't we been formulating this plan for, oh . . . the past century? The others will return to us if they can."

"And if they can't?" she asked. "What happens to them?"

"Do you really think I care?"

It took Piper close to an hour to get home from the financial district because streetlights and traffic lights were out all over the city. The pouring rain didn't help any, nor did the general populace's tendency to shy away from giving the right of way when everyone came to a four-way stop at an intersection. The one good thing about the rain was that it was helping control some of the fires that had sprung up. The quake hadn't been as bad as the big one that hit back when Piper was in high school, but it was fairly substantial.

Piper and Muriel kept their conversation to a minimum so Piper could concentrate on driving through the obstacle course of torn-up streets, abandoned cars, and windblown debris. They found that there was suddenly a lot less to say as they took in the destruction, knowing things would only get worse if Tempest managed to get a hold of the Elementals' powers before combining together to form the body of Piper's orbing husband.

"That's a neat little trick," Muriel said as Leo became whole.

"Company?" Leo asked as he held out his hand to Muriel. "Hi, I'm Leo."

"Muriel," she replied as she took his hand. "You'll have to show me how you do that sometime."

"Sorry, it's kind of one of those innate things," he said.

"Pity," she replied, letting go of his hand but allowing her eyes to linger a moment.

Piper wasn't sure, but she thought that the senior citizen was coming on to her husband.

"The house looks a lot worse up there," Leo said to Piper as he took in the surroundings and Muriel.

"Hey, I had nothing to do with it," Muriel said, holding her hands up in an innocent pose.

"I take it Muriel is the Earthshaker," he said as he righted a chair so she could sit.

"Guilty," Muriel said, taking the seat.

"Since you know her title, I'm assuming the Elders were a help?" Piper asked, trying to keep the surprise out of her voice. More often than not, the all-powerful beings that watched over the Charmed Ones liked to let them figure things out for themselves. Leo, being the conduit to the Elders, usually got stuck in the middle of those struggles of will.

"Is that why it took you so long to orb home?" Leo asked.

Paige and Rafe exchanged a look.

"Not exactly," he said.

"You know where you don't want to be during an earthquake?" Paige asked, but didn't wait for an answer. "You don't want to be in a zoo . . . or anywhere *near* a zoo, for that matter."

Everyone in the room got their own mental picture of what Paige was suggesting.

"We decided to stick around for a while and help corral the animals," Paige said. "Once that seemed to be in hand, we left Rafe's truck in the parking lot and zipped right back here."

"That little transporter thing was fun," Rafe said. "And would be so convenient when I'm late for work."

"Any word on Darryl or Phoebe?" Paige asked.

"Nope," Piper replied as she got up to start pacing. She knew her sister could handle herself well enough, but worrying was what big sisters did best.

"Maybe we should go over what we know so far," Leo suggested.

Piper assumed that he said that to help take her mind off whatever Phoebe may be up to. She appreciated the suggestion, but she could talk and worry at the same time.

The group followed Piper's lead, bringing everyone up to speed and contributing where they could. Rafe seemed to be having the most

"She's kind of an . . . intensely focused individual," Phoebe explained. "I mean, she quit her job as a lawyer to pursue a medical career. Can you believe that? And here I thought I'd be stuck working on the newspaper for the rest of my life."

"I'm sorry," Muriel said, working up a little head of steam. "But I'm sixty-seven . . . I've had *five* careers . . . and I'm not even ready for retirement yet. What's the big deal? I understand this woman's busy, but she's got to make time."

"Like going out of town right before a hugely important ritual?" Piper asked, trying to keep an accusatory tone out of her voice. In truth, she was a little jealous since she couldn't remember the last time *she* had gotten out of town.

"Yes," Muriel said. "Aside from the Night of Aeolus, my family has always tried to use our powers to help mankind. But in addition to that, we have also tried to live our lives. And the first thing we're taught is how to prioritize and find time for ourselves. Haven't you girls learned that yet?"

Piper wasn't sure that she got the point. "But you said you wished you could have been here earlier," she reminded Muriel.

"But the truth is, I probably couldn't have stopped anything that happened," Muriel said. "And I would have been in the same danger as Christopher, so it was really for the best that I was in L.A."

"Gabrielle," Phoebe added, then mumbled, "if we can get her."

"—and then Leo and Paige can orb us over there," she finished.

"No can do, honey," Leo said. "The Elders said that we had to get to the Circle of Gaea by earthly means."

"Earthly means?" Piper asked. "What exactly does that mean? Can we take my car?"

"I know a few people who might not consider an SUV to be very 'earthly,'" Phoebe said.

"Well, if we have to walk there we're already too late," Leo said.

"What about that 'by the light of the moon,' part you guys mentioned earlier?" Rafe asked.

Piper glanced out the window to see that the storm was still raging. *Good question,* she thought. She also noticed that the FBI agents had left, probably after the quake hit.

"Don't worry about the moon thing," Muriel said. "Everything will be fine once we get there. Oh, there is one thing I almost forgot. We're going to need a few items for the ritual."

"Such as?" Piper asked.

"A sword, a wand, a chalice, and some coins," Muriel replied. "Preferably old coins. The time period doesn't really matter, but the older the better."

"We've got all that in the attic," Piper said.

Rafe looked at Paige curiously. "You've got a very interesting family," he said.

Chapter

15

Everyone in the room froze when they heard the concern in Leo's voice. Piper immediately regretted leaving Darryl to look after Tyler with no defenses against demon attack.

"Okay . . . ," Leo said into the phone. He looked at the sisters. "Paige is already on her way to your house, so she should be there in a couple of minutes. Do you need a ride to the hospital?"

The Charmed Ones took a collective breath and stood up. The guests in the room had no doubt that these were sisters by the way they moved as one to Leo's side.

"I understand . . . ," Leo continued. "We'll meet you there."

"Hospital?" Piper asked as Leo hung up the phone. "Was there an attack? How's Tyler?"

"No attack," Leo said calmly. "Tyler's fine.

"Honey?" Leo took his wife in his arms.

"Go," Piper said calmly, yet forcefully.

Leo let go of his wife, took Phoebe by the arm, and did as he was told.

Piper watched as they disappeared. She was on the verge of tears. Sure, they had been through worse before, but Darryl was injured over an hour ago. There was no telling whether or not Leo would make it in time.

"I'll get the things we need for the ritual," she said without looking at her houseguests and made her way to the stairs.

When Piper reached the attic she realized that she had forgotten about the blown-out door. It seemed like ages ago since they'd vanquished the demon that had tried to take Tyler's power.

The plastic sheeting Leo had put up over the broken window in the attic was flapping in the wind as rain poured inside. She hurried over to the window and reattached the plastic to the nails Leo had put in the walls. It probably wouldn't hold for much longer, but there were more pressing concerns than the attic floor getting wet.

Piper turned and went over to the trunk where she and her sisters stored the odd weapons they collected in their travels. There were several swords inside, and she chose the most lightweight one, figuring it would be easier to carry to the Circle of Gaea.

The chalice and wand were the next things on her mental list. They were easy enough to locate

"I can see that," Muriel said. "Everything is going to work out."

"How can you say that?" Piper asked, banging more drawers.

"Because it always does," Muriel replied.

Piper slammed the last drawer shut. "No, it doesn't," she said quietly, thinking back to her sister Prue, who had died the last time everything *didn't* work out.

"True," Muriel said as something unspoken passed between the two of them. "But we move on. We live. And honey, you've got to live."

"But I've got all these responsibilities . . . ," Piper said.

"And you do what you can and then move on. Start by finding anything that can make your life a little easier," Muriel said as she held out her hand and showed Piper that she was holding two quarters, a dime, and four pennies. "Rafe had these in his pocket."

"But you said you needed old coins," Piper said.

"No, I said that old coins would be *better*," Muriel corrected her. "But if it's going to take us all night to find those coins, we should just make do with what we have. It doesn't always have to be perfect. It just has to be good enough."

Piper's mind flashed back to her Mulligatawny stew.

Paige orbed herself right to Darryl's front door and rang the bell. Sheila had it open almost

"Go," Shelia said, pushing them toward the kitchen. "Out the back door. The last thing Darryl needs when he wakes up is to be questioned about what a missing child was doing in his home."

Even though Sheila was speaking logically, with no accusatory tone in her voice, Paige couldn't help but think that she was being blamed. She chose not to say anything as she and Tyler went back out into the rain. As soon as the door was shut, Paige orbed them home.

In the blink of an eye they were back in the living room. Rafe was sitting on the couch alone.

"Where'd everybody go?" Paige asked.

"Leo and Phoebe are at the hospital," Rafe explained, looking down at Tyler. "Piper and Muriel are upstairs."

"Tyler, this is Rafe," Paige said. "You two have something in common. Rafe can control the wind, and he just found that out this afternoon. So, your little eleven-year-old self is way ahead of him."

Rafe and Tyler shook hands awkwardly— the boy was obviously uncomfortable with the adult ritual. Once again, though, they felt a ripple of energy go through the air as Fire and Air met.

"You know, I think we have some ice cream in the kitchen," Paige said. "Mint chocolate chip."

"Hot chocolate, mac and cheese, and ice cream," Tyler said, reliving his junk food intake. "All in one day."

"You should get kidnapped more often, huh?" Paige said before she realized the words were out

"I've found my calling," Paige said. "I'm a witch, remember?"

"No, that's your mission," Rafe said. "Your calling is something that you want to do, not something that you *have* to do."

"Right now, I *have* to focus on my magic," Paige said as she closed the ice cream container and put it back in the freezer.

"But that doesn't mean you have to give up entirely on your calling," Rafe countered. "It just means you have to postpone it for a while. Don't worry, it'll come when you need it."

Paige considered what he was saying . . . and wondered why she'd chosen to stop flirting with him earlier.

Leo and Phoebe paced outside the operating room that was off to the side of the ER. They had been at the hospital for fifteen minutes and had gotten little information so far.

"What's going on in there?" Phoebe asked.

"The nurse said the wound was deep," Leo reminded her. "This kind of surgery can't be rushed."

"Well, you can't save him if he dies on the operating table," Phoebe said in exasperation. "We should have brought Piper. She could have frozen time so we could slip in there."

"And miraculously heal him in the middle of the operation?" Leo asked. "I don't think the Elders would like that plan."

"I'll go look for her," Phoebe said as she left Leo.

Even though the place was packed, it didn't take her long to find Gabrielle. The woman was comforting a little girl who was holding her arm like it was broken. Phoebe waited for Gabrielle to walk away before approaching her.

"Hey, Gabby," Phoebe said, forcing the cheeriness into her voice.

"It's *Gabrielle*," she replied, sounding exhausted. "Look, I know I told you to come back later, but as you can see, it's crazy here. I just can't go."

"Yeah, we'll get to that in a minute," Phoebe said. "First I need you to come with me."

"I've got patients to look after," Gabrielle said.

"Yeah, and I've got a specific one who needs your help," Phoebe said as she pulled the med student along with her.

When they reached Leo, Phoebe saw by the look on his face that he had some news.

"The operation's over," Leo said before she could even introduce him to Gabrielle. "But he's still in critical condition. There's a nurse in there, but she won't let me in."

"Gabrielle, we need you to get the nurse out in the hall," Phoebe said.

"Look, you and your friend have to understand that the nurse has a job to do," Gabrielle explained. "And so do I. You just can't get in the way."

"Yes, we can," Phoebe said simply. "We're trying to save a life."

"And we need her to stay away for a few minutes," Leo said. "She can't come right back or—"

"Why don't I just offer to take over for her?" Gabrielle said simply, in a somewhat condescending tone.

"You can do that?" Phoebe asked, surprised by the ease of the plan.

"I'm a medical student," Gabrielle reminded them. "That's why I'm here . . . to help."

Phoebe knew when she was being berated, so she shut her mouth as Gabrielle entered Darryl's room. She found the woman to be an interesting case. Rarely had she seen a person so focused on her goals. *It's a shame that it keeps her from seeing that whole big picture thing*, Phoebe thought.

The nurse left about a minute after Gabrielle went into the room. Phoebe and Leo exchanged a look and waited for the nurse to disappear down the hall before going in.

"Your friend's in bad shape," Gabrielle said quickly. She obviously still needed to work on that bedside manner.

"It's okay," Phoebe said as she looked over Darryl, who appeared to be far from okay. "As long as he's alive."

"I can work with that," Leo completed the thought as he moved to the bed.

"What are you going to do?" Gabrielle asked.

"Just watch," Phoebe said as she took her own advice.

Darryl looked across the room, both happy to see his wife and upset that he had caused her to worry.

"Hi, dear," he said. "Don't worry. I'm—"

Sheila cut him off by crossing the room in two giant steps and throwing him into a tight hug. The embrace ached a little, as he still wasn't a hundred percent over being almost dead.

"You scared me," she said as she pulled away from him and playfully smacked him.

Darryl considered acting like she had really hurt him, but figured that joke might be just a little cruel. Besides, he needed her in a good mood for the discussion they were about to have.

"Um . . . we'll wait outside," Phoebe said as she pushed Leo out of the room.

"I have to stay and monitor the equipment," Gabrielle shyly explained. "Although I'm thinking that's not entirely necessary now."

"You can stay," Darryl said. "I don't want you to get into trouble for abandoning your post." He turned his gaze to his wife. "How's Darryl Junior? Did he ride out the quake?"

"He's fine," Sheila replied. "Having a wonderful time with his grandparents. But how are you? Really."

"Just a little tingle in my chest," Darryl said, rubbing the spot where he had been injured. "Otherwise, I'm perfectly fine."

"Good," Sheila said with relief. "Now what's this about you going somewhere?"

miss me," Darryl said, "especially if my wife raises some hell over getting me out of here."

"Somehow I doubt that," Sheila said, looking over to Gabrielle for confirmation.

The medical student just shrugged.

"I'll see what I can do," Sheila said, giving him another hug. "Don't you go anywhere until I get back."

"Where can I go?" Darryl asked, pointing to his blankets and thin hospital gown. "I'm naked under this flimsy hospital gown."

"Don't remind me," Sheila said in a flirtatious tone.

Now Darryl felt *really* embarrassed that someone else was in the room.

"You know they're not going to release you," Gabrielle said as soon as Sheila was out of the room. "The doctors don't even know you're awake."

"It's not like they can stop me," Darryl said. "Can I get a little help here?" He indicated to the wires and tubes attached at various points along his body.

Gabrielle hesitated for a moment before giving in and unhooking him from everything.

"Besides, they're probably preoccupied by the quake," he said once he was free. "How bad was it?"

"Bad enough," she replied.

"Well, we'll take care of that," he said as he went over to get his pants, which were hanging wait outside? You could have come back in when Sheila left."

"We wanted to give you and Gabrielle a chance to talk," Phoebe replied, looking at the med student. "Did Darryl convince you to come along?"

Gabrielle looked at her for a moment. "How did you know?"

Phoebe threw a smile in Darryl's direction. "Because that's what Darryl does."

maternal. "You could put your whole face out with that thing."

"I'll be careful," Tyler said. "Promise."

Piper considered the request. It might be incredibly wrong to arm a normal child that way, but she also knew that he had already proven he was mature enough for the responsibility.

"Okay," she gave in, handing him the sword. "But only use it for the ritual. Don't go swinging it around . . . unless you absolutely have to."

"Cool," Tyler said as he held the sword in his hands. Piper could tell that he was just dying to hack at something.

How sweet, she thought sarcastically. Then she handed the wand to Rafe.

"First person who makes a Harry Potter joke gets it," Rafe said, holding the wand up menacingly. "Right between the eyes."

Piper completed her task of handing out the symbolic ritual items by giving Gabrielle the chalice that her Grams used to say she drank from at her third wedding. Muriel already had the sixty-four cents safely in her pocket.

"Whoa, somebody looks hot," Phoebe said as Darryl and Leo came down the stairs.

"Thank you," Leo said, modestly.

Piper knew that her sister was referring to Darryl, who had borrowed one of Leo's shirts. It was a little tight on the police officer and showed off his well-developed muscles. Although, Piper and was met with a round of nodding heads. The tension was stronger than the ripple of power that seemed to be emanating from the Elementals every few minutes. Only hours earlier Rafe, Gabrielle, and even Tyler had no clue of the huge responsibilities on their shoulders.

"You okay?" Phoebe asked as she took a seat on the couch beside Gabrielle.

"Just a little overwhelmed," Gabrielle replied. "This wasn't part of my plan. You see . . . I have a very specific life plan ensuring that I make the best use of my time."

"I think saving the world is a pretty good use of your time," Phoebe said, trying to figure the woman out.

"It is," Gabrielle said. "But it's not part of the plan. I mean, what do I do next? If this works out, I mean. I guess we're all dead if it doesn't, so that will be a pretty definite plan. But I mean, I've got this power that I never expected to have. Am I like a superhero?"

Phoebe was amazed to watch this incredibly put-together, totally ordered and precise woman break down right in front of her.

"No, you're not a superhero," Phoebe said, although she often wondered the same thing about herself. "You're just a person with a gift. It's up to you whether or not you choose to embrace it. You can't plan for everything, you know. Eventually something will come up that could

"Well, then my life is just a three-ring circus," Paige said. "Anyway, Gabrielle's like this totally obsessive-compulsive planner—"

"Yeah. Couldn't tell," Rafe said sarcastically.

"Anyway," Paige continued. "I think you were right earlier. I should just plan to focus on my magic for a while and worry about where my life will take me later."

"Doesn't take a house to fall on you," he said.

"That was a witch joke, wasn't it?" Paige said, smirking.

Piper was in the kitchen with Tyler making sure he ate something other than junk food before facing demons. The young Firestarter downed the last of his turkey sandwich and finished off a second glass of milk.

"Thanks," he said as he headed back toward his new friends in the living room.

"You're welcome," Piper replied. "Don't forget your sword."

"Why does he bring that sword everywhere?" asked Muriel, who had wandered into the kitchen also looking for a snack.

"I chose to leave the question unasked," Piper replied.

"Good call," Muriel said. "I think you'll make a great mother someday. Any plans?"

"Plans, yes," Piper replied. "Success, no."

"Keep at it," Muriel said with a gleam in her eye. "I'm sure something will happen soon enough."

Chapter
18

The group left in two cars, uncomfortable with the risks involved in orbing back and forth to get everyone to Crystal Springs Reservoir; they weren't sure just how far the edict to "travel by earthly means" extended and didn't want to take their chances. Based on their earlier drives through the city, they gave themselves two hours to get to the Circle of Gaea, which they figured was more than enough time to get there and set up, taking into account any possible demon battling they may have to do.

Piper drove her SUV with Leo, Tyler, Darryl, and Muriel. At Muriel's suggestion, they sang car travel songs as they made their way slowly through the streets of town. Piper had assumed that it was Muriel's way of keeping Tyler calm, but, as he had called shotgun, she could see that he looked rather bored by it all. Muriel, on the was just looking for a reason to be annoyed.

It took Paige almost a half hour to realize that Rafe wasn't really interested in Gabrielle. He was just fooling around to see if he could get the woman to laugh. Paige figured it out when he caught her eye in the rearview mirror and made a face at her.

Paige also saw Gabrielle give her a strange look when she started laughing out loud for no apparent reason.

"You know, you could probably stop all this rain if you really wanted to," Rafe said. "I mean, it is only water."

"No, actually it's a combination of climatic factors occurring all around us and affecting the clouds thousands of feet in the air above, only then resulting in the water all around us," Gabrielle clarified.

"I knew you could be fun at parties," Rafe said. "Look at all the useless trivia you have at your disposal for small talk."

"Maybe you could at least hold back the rain between Piper and us. I can hardly see the SUV," Paige said. She played along with Rafe not just because it was fun, but because she could really use the help. It had gotten easier to navigate since there was hardly any traffic on the road out here, but it was totally dark and almost impossible to see Piper's taillights in the downpour.

"I don't really know how to do that," Gabrielle said, sounding like she was disappointed with her lack of knowledge.

could not get the traction it needed. Instead of sliding off the road and down the embankment, it launched itself into the air, using the upturned road as a ramp.

"No!" Piper yelled.

It was as if the strength of her voice had developed a new magical power, because Phoebe's car slammed to a halt mid-air. Piper realized that Rafe must have used his powers as the car rocked from side to side, being buffeted by the winds.

Piper and the others jumped out of the SUV into the rainy night.

"Why aren't they coming down?" Tyler asked as the car started thrashing in mid-air.

"Rafe can't control it!" Muriel yelled.

"Everybody back!" Leo shouted over the increasing winds.

The group ran across the deserted road and watched in horror as the car flipped upside down and kept jumping wildly.

"Leo, do something," Piper shouted over the winds.

Her husband didn't have a chance to act as four sets of sparkly light appeared in front of them. A moment later Paige appeared with Phoebe, Rafe, and Gabrielle, holding hands.

"Let it down gently," Phoebe pleaded, still holding her keys which had been orbed right out of the ignition as she shut off the car in midair.

But Rafe was still not in control.

"Great," Paige said. "And in the pouring rain too."

"I think I can do something about that," Gabrielle said as she closed her eyes and started concentrating.

"Remember," Phoebe said, catching on to the plan. "Feel it, don't think."

Gabrielle opened her eyes, and when she did, the rain stopped. Well, it still kept coming down, but once it was about three feet over their heads—Darryl's head to be specific since he was the tallest—it divided like the Red Sea and came down around the group.

"We have to stay close," Gabrielle said. "I can't push the rain too far."

"You're doing fine," Muriel said.

"I could probably dry us all off," Tyler eagerly suggested. "All I have to do is focus my power."

"That's okay," Piper said. She figured that Tyler just wanted to feel like he was contributing, but she wasn't ready to put her clothes—and her body—at the mercy of his flames. "But we could use some light."

"Why don't you try a small fireball about three feet in front of us," Muriel suggested.

Tyler seemed to like the idea and let his emotions cast a little ball of fire to light their way. He tried to take the lead position, but Piper pulled him back into the mix, since it was a little dangerous for him to be front and center. She allowed her husband to take that position.

But Darryl *was* worried. It was unlikely that Tempest would know the location for the ritual, since none of them had known it either. However, Darryl was getting used to how the demon mind worked and how they always seemed to have a surprise or two up their sleeves. That's exactly why he put himself on high alert when the rain stopped entirely.

He looked up and saw the clear moonlit sky above him, but that wasn't the surprising part. It was still a downpour only three feet behind him.

"Did I do that?" Gabrielle asked, almost in awe of herself.

"No, sweetie," Muriel said. "We've reached the trail."

Darryl saw that she was right. There was a trail cut into the trees on the side of the road. But he liked that path even less. On the road they had at least had some warning if something was about to attack them. The trees provided a frightening amount of cover even though the sky lit the path well enough that Tyler could put out his guiding fire.

"I don't like this," Darryl said, looking into the trees.

"I think we're all in agreement on that one," Paige said.

Muriel pushed a tiny button on her watch and the face glowed for a moment. "Well, like it or not, we've got to get moving. It's getting on midnight."

Chapter 19

Darryl's shock wore off quickly as his instincts took over, and he came back slamming his fist in the demon's face.

"Stay back," Darryl warned as he saw the female demon appear in the center of the clearing. If the male demon had appeared like that it was no wonder he was able to get the drop on Darryl.

The woman raised her hand to show she was carrying a weapon.

"Gun!" Paige yelled, and she orbed the weapon to her a moment after it was fired. It was still hot when the barrel landed in her hand, forcing her to drop it on the ground.

The rest of the group dove for cover as the lone bullet crossed the clearing toward them. Piper pulled Tyler down with her as she froze the bullet before it hit Leo.

could. He took off his jacket, wrapped it around his fist, and gave the demon a blunted yet powerful hit across the chin. It knocked the demon off Tyler, but the heat from the power transfer was so intense that it set Darryl's jacket on fire, burning his hand. He managed to burn his free hand too, trying to remove the flaming clothes.

Leo took the opportunity to reclaim the sword and thrust it through the demon's chest.

At the same time, Phoebe was looking to be evenly matched with the female. Every kick Phoebe landed was blocked or countered. Even her power to levitate could not serve her as the demon clamped on to ensure that Phoebe couldn't get the upper hand.

Phoebe managed to shake the demon loose, but was distracted when Tyler ran into the clearing. The demon used that to her advantage as she grabbed Phoebe's leg and flung her, hard, to the ground.

Paige was right behind her sister with a vanquishing potion at the ready. Unfortunately, the demon didn't give her the chance to throw it as she attacked. Paige's fighting skills were as not as honed as her sister's, but she managed to land a few good blows before the demon knocked her aside, smashing the potion bottle in the process.

Once her partner was killed, the female wasted no time finishing the job he had started. She hurried across the clearing and grabbed on to Tyler, holding him like a shield in front of her.

The demon's eyes went wide.

"Now!" Paige yelled.

Muriel, Rafe, and Gabrielle grabbed hands and let loose with their powers, focusing on the demon holding Tyler. But the ground did not shake, the winds did not blow, and the rain did not fall. Instead, the three of them followed Muriel's unspoken guidance and hit the demon with their raw power, shooting beams of brown, sky blue, and aqua light from their bodies.

"No!" the demon screamed as she absorbed the full effects of the fire, water, air, and wind together. The intensity forced her to drop Tyler to the ground, but even with one less power entering her body it still proved too much. The demon exploded above Tyler, sending smoke up through the trees.

Silence fell over the clearing once again.

"That was *so* cool!" Tyler said as he picked himself up off the ground.

"That kid has a weird idea of fun," Paige said.

"Seemed pretty cool to me," Rafe agreed.

"Speak for yourself," Darryl said as he cringed over his burned hands.

"Here, let me," Leo said as he took Darryl's hands in his and worked his healing power.

"Couldn't do this in a more manly way, could you?" Darryl asked as they held hands. "Maybe over a couple beers."

"Next time," Leo said.

"After being healed twice in one day, I don't

from the group. Not quite diminutive, but certainly not as imposing as his minions had been in person. Then again, his minions weren't very imposing anymore either.

"You know," Piper said as she stepped into the clearing, "considering your minions didn't have any powers of their own, I'm guessing you don't have any either."

"You'd be correct," Tempest said from his spot in the center of the stone.

Piper was surprised that he had answered her so readily.

"And without those minions to act as a conduit for the power," Phoebe added, "I'm guessing you have no way to drain the Elementals directly."

"That would be true as well," Tempest replied.

"So, then you're not really a threat anymore?" Paige added.

"Well, I could always kill you and force the Elementals to give me their power during the ritual," Tempest said.

"And how could you do that?" Piper took up the questioning again.

Paige used the fact her sister had the demon's attention to pull two potion bottles out of her bag. She handed one to Phoebe.

"I may not *own* their powers," Tempest said. "But as long as I stand in the Circle of Gaea, I can *control* them."

Paige and Phoebe each threw the vanquishing

sending the Charmed Ones to their knees and Muriel to the ground as he stole her control of the earth.

Surprisingly, it was Gabrielle who tried to beat Tempest to the punch by willing a flood of water out of the nearby reservoir, but Tempest effortlessly sent it back at her, knocking her to the ground.

While Tempest's focus was split attempting to control the four powers at once, the Charmed Ones locked hands again and tried to work their spell once more. But the combination of wind carrying their words and the water flooding their mouths stopped them.

Tempest was so consumed with drowning the witches on dry land that he didn't notice the mortal sneaking up on him until Darryl launched himself at the demon and pulled him off the Circle of Gaea.

As Darryl landed on the grass with the demon he yelled to the Charmed Ones, "Now!"

Piper, Phoebe, and Paige stood and clasped hands, reciting the spell they had prepared earlier.

> *By the Water and the Air,*
> *By the Earth and the Fire,*
> *By the powers that we bear,*
> *Tempest's life, now expire.*

Darryl rolled off the demon as his body glowed a bright aqua, then shifted slightly to

"The most powerful Elemental there is," Muriel said. "It is the one that holds all the other elements together: the *Human* Spirit."

"What are you talking about?" Piper asked as she checked her own watch to see there were only two minutes to midnight. "You didn't say anything about finding a Human Spirit."

"Didn't have to," Muriel said. "You've had a very powerful one with you all day. The only full human in the group . . . Darryl, will you please take your spot on the circle?"

"Muriel, why didn't it say anything about a Spirit Elemental in Christopher's files?" Piper asked, though Darryl suspected she was just stalling to give him time to accept the fact that the ritual apparently hinged on him.

"It's not the Firestarter's responsibility to find the Spirit Elemental," Muriel explained. "The Spirit is the one who finds the Firestarter."

Well, technically, my job was *to find the Firestarter*, Darryl thought. *And I managed to do that quickly enough.*

He looked down at the sword, chalice, wand, and coins that were lying at the feet of their respective Elementals.

"But I don't have a symbol of my power," Darryl said, this time providing his own stalling.

"Of course you do," Muriel said as she stepped off the stone and moved toward Darryl. "Your symbol is heart." She gently guided him into his position. "Now let's get this puppy started."

Darryl watched the Charmed Ones and their Whitelighter step away from the circle to give the Elementals space to perform the ritual. He wasn't sure what he had to do since he had missed that part of the briefing—what with being near death. Darryl just followed along as the Elementals joined hands by taking Gabrielle's on his left and Tyler's on his right.

"Tyler," Muriel said.

"Now?" Tyler asked.

She smiled and gave him a nod.

danced in front of them, then exploded up to the sky in a brilliant burst.

Once again the clearing was lit solely by moonlight.

"The Earth is at peace," Muriel said.

"Really?" Rafe asked. "Doesn't feel any different."

The clearing was exactly the same as it had been before the ritual. The only difference that Darryl noticed was a gentle breeze replacing the eerie stillness that had been there before.

"Oh, but it is," Muriel said calmly, then broke her serious demeanor and looked at Tyler. "Race you back to the car."

The boy apparently considered taking off, but stopped himself when he realized the woman was making a joke.

Paige considered the day's events as the group made their way back on the path to the road. She understood exactly what Tyler, Rafe, Gabrielle, and even Darryl were going through emotionally after finding out that they each had an unexpected gift that they could use to do such important work.

As she and the group came out of the woods, the first thing they noticed was that the sky was just as clear as it had been above the Circle of Gaea and the wind just as gentle.

"Wow," said Tyler. After all they'd been through it was pretty much all anyone could say.

alone since she had pulled in several spots away
from the truck.

"Phoebe's not too big with the subtle," Rafe
said as they took the short stroll to the truck he
had borrowed.

"Not so much," Paige agreed. "Look, I—"

"Hey, I get it," Rafe interrupted. "Believe
me, I totally understand needing some time for
yourself."

"It's not permanent," Paige said. "I just want
to figure out what I'm doing with my work and
my magic . . . and ultimately the rest of my life."

"And why would you want to get involved
with a guy who has well over two dozen kids in
various parts of the city?" Rafe asked.

Paige's eyes nearly bugged out.

"Schoolteacher . . . remember?" he said,
beaming a smile at her.

"It's been a long day," Paige said, shaking her
head.

"Well . . . good-bye," Rafe said as they did the
awkward "handshake or kiss" dance.

Mid-step, Paige noticed a strange paw print
on the hood of Rafe's car, "What do you think
that is?"

"Either a monkey or a duck-billed platypus,"
Rafe said. "I'm sure a few of the animals took the
quake as their chance to escape."

"I think duck-billed platypuses . . . or platypi?"
Paige wondered. "They have webbed feet."

"I know," Rafe said. "I just wanted to hear

"One step at a time, Phoebe," Gabrielle replied. "One step at a time."

The streets were fairly clear so late at night. Now that the storm had subsided, the damage from the quake didn't seem as bad as it had when the heavy winds were blowing debris around. The city had even managed to get most of the lights back on between the zoo and the hospital, which were not all that close to each other.

"Here we are," Phoebe said as she pulled in by the emergency room entrance.

"Thanks," Gabrielle said as she got out of the car. "For everything."

"You did the hard part," Paige said with a wave.

"Still, I feel that somehow I need to thank you," Gabrielle said. "For getting me to accept who I am."

"Forget about it," Paige said. "We do this kind of thing every day."

"Not so fast," Phoebe said as she looked up at the former lawyer from the driver's seat. "Gabrielle, how are you with contracts?"

Piper couldn't help but be excited as she and Darryl followed Tyler up the walk to his house. The door was locked so he started ringing the bell frantically and banging on the door. The noise echoed through the quiet neighborhood, but Piper didn't stop him. It was nice to see him so quick to return to his normal life.

She had given Tyler another drink of the

"They're entirely out of the picture," Darryl said. "Tyler will be fine."

Piper couldn't help but wonder if that was true. She had thought Tyler was safe the last time she had bound his powers. It was all the more reason she would have to look in on him from time to time.

"What happened?" Stephen asked, apparently wanting more of an explanation.

"Not now, Stephen," Maria said, hugging her son. "In the morning. Tyler looks exhausted."

Thanks for the save, Piper thought.

"We should get going," Darryl said. "Let you have your reunion and get Tyler to bed."

Tyler broke from his mom and gave Piper a big good-bye hug that really tugged at those maternal urges.

"Thanks for everything, Piper," he said as he let go. "You too, Darryl." He took the officer's hand and gave him a very manly shake.

"You were pretty impressive there yourself," Darryl said. "Don't forget, I'm going to need a babysitter sometime. Maybe next weekend when I have to make up for missing a night out with my wife."

Piper gave both the parents a hug good-bye, while Darryl kept it to a more professional handshake. They both took a deep breath as the front door closed behind them and they walked to the SUV.

"So, what exactly are you going to write in

"Hey, you were the one just hugging the big guy here," Muriel said, giving Darryl a playful slap on the back.

"I guess it will be okay," Piper said, acting like she was skeptical over the whole idea.

Leo and Darryl kindly stepped aside so the two women could say a proper good-bye.

"Thanks for all the help, kiddo," Muriel said. "The little Firestarter couldn't have done it without you."

"I had a lot of help," Piper reminded her.

"Still, you were the one in charge," Muriel said. "Trust me. In my life I've overseen hundreds, if not thousands of employees. You made that look downright simple compared to everything you handled today."

"Maybe I should tackle that stew again," Piper joked. "We never had dinner."

"Maybe you should go romance that hunky husband of yours," Muriel said with a wink. "The stew can wait."

Piper liked that idea better than standing over a stew pot again. There would be time for that later.

They exchanged good-byes and Piper moved over with Darryl to watch Leo and Muriel orb away. They both stood in silence a moment longer, still absorbing all that had happened throughout the day.

"Let's get you home," Piper finally said.

faint glow that turned out to be candlelight.

Two white taper candles were lit on either side of the table. Sheila's favorite table linens and the fine china and crystal had been laid out under the glow of the candles. Darryl was glad to see that none of it had been damaged in the earthquake.

"Welcome home," Sheila said as she came in from the kitchen wearing her black silk robe and carrying a covered tray. She walked over to the table, put down the tray, and turned to give her husband a kiss.

"What's all this?" he asked.

"I realize your day was crazy," she replied. "But don't tell me you forgot all about our romantic dinner."

In that moment, Darryl loved his wife more than he thought possible.

"Voilà," she said as she removed the cover from the tray to reveal a pair of peanut butter and jelly sandwiches. "I didn't want to use the gas oven in case another aftershock hit."

Darryl knew that was no longer a concern, but he didn't care. They could have a romantic meal over a couple of Pez candies. He took his wife in his arms again and slowly swayed to the music.

"I'm sorry," he said as they danced. "I—"

"Not tonight," Sheila replied. "I know your life is crazy. I don't want to make it any crazier."

"Thank you," he said.

About the Author

Paul Ruditis has written and contributed to various books based on such notable TV shows as *Buffy the Vampire Slayer; Sabrina, The Teenage Witch; The West Wing; Star Trek: Voyager;* and *Enterprise.* He lives in Burbank, California.